Protecting Chanel

A One Nightstand Bodyguard Romance

TN Nashville Division
Book 2

KeKe Renée

Chiquita Dennie

304 Publishing Company

Latest Releases By Keke Renée:

By Keke Renée:
Wet Heat
Every Time We Touch (A Wet Heat Novelette)
His Peace, Her Pleasure
Baby, It's Cold Outside
Love Don't Live Here Anymore (Andrew sisters) Book 1
Love Don't Live Here Anymore (Andrew sisters) Book 2
One Night Only-A Novelette
Deidra's Love
Haven
Seek To Please
Seek To Touch
Seek To Bare
Seek To Love
Seek To Trust
Seek To Earn
Tease Me Book 1
Promise Me Book 2

Consume Me Book 3

Claim Me Book 4

Tempt Me Book 5

Ravage Me Book 6

Sensual

Protecting Bria (TN Seal Security Nashville Division Book 1)

Protecting Chanel (TN Seal Security Nashville Division Book 2)

Protecting Yanira (TN Seal Security Nashville Division Book 3)

Note To Readers:

Protecting Chanel is revamped from previously being published in another author's world. Same story with updated characters, partner series of the original Memphis TN Seal Security series.

I WANT TO THANK FIRST the readers for loving these characters so much and waiting so long for them to come back.

Disclaimer

THIS WORK OF FICTION has some parts made up, like locations, even though it takes place in Nashville, for the main backdrop. Contains strong language and explicit sexual content and is only intended for mature readers. This story may contain unconventional situations, language, and sexual encounters that may offend some readers. This book is for mature readers (18+).

Introduction

Grab some wine and get ready for spicy, sinful, sexy fun with Maddux, Chanel, and the team from TN SEAL Security Nashville Division.

Are you signed up for my newsletter?

Join today and find out all the latest in new releases, contests, giveaways, sneak peeks, and more.

Synopsis

When a fun yacht trip turns into a nightmare at sea, her only hope is the Navy SEAL she tried to forget.

Chanel

I deserve a break, or at least that's what my friend says. So, I agree to join her to relax on a yacht. The plan was to have fun and unwind, perhaps even flirt a little, not get caught up in an on-board fling with the sexiest man I've ever laid eyes on.

Maddux

I had a fling I can't forget and probably won't ever see again. So, imagine my surprise when I'm assigned as her bodyguard after she reveals an unexpected surprise. But the flames we felt when we first met haven't dimmed and soon we're falling into each other's arms again. I've sworn to keep her safe, risking my life to do so, and when a threat takes her from me, I lay it all on the line—including my heart.

Grab your copy of Protecting Chanel now and indulge in a romantic suspense unlike anything you've ever read. If you enjoy military romances, damsels in distress, forced proximity, and steamy romance, then this is a series you don't want to miss.

Chapter 1

Chanel

I blew my hair away from my eyes and stared at the two outfits I wanted to bring with me on this trip. It was the weekend, and I had time off work to finally hang with my friends, chill, and have some drinks. Maybe I'd have a little fun with the sexy guy Rose told me would be there. Unable to decide, I grabbed both the dress and the shorts outfit and put them in my bag. Rose would probably curse me out for being late, but this would be my last vacation for a while because my job wanted me to open another office location.

"Makeup!" I snapped my fingers and ran to grab my makeup case off the vanity, placing it in my bag. Glancing in the mirror, I turned to look at my ass in the shorts and the loose top that hung off one shoulder. Rose recommended this new body oil, and it had my magenta rich skin tone glowing. At thirty, living in Nashville, making a six-figure income, and with a great head on my shoulders, I was now focused on finding love.

Honk!

"Coming!" I shouted, grabbing my purse and bag of clothes, and slid my feet in light brown sandals.

I rubbed the top of my dog's head, picked her up, and laid her on the couch with my neighbor's daughter, Rutina. She'd been my longtime person for dog-sitting.

"Princess, be good for me, okay?"

I took out a hundred bucks and placed it in her hand. "Rutina, if you need anything, remember to call me." Right on time my cell vibrated, and I slipped it out of my pocket and read a message from Rose.

"I will. Have fun." Rutina waved, and I kissed the top of Princess' head again. My baby was my family, next to Rose and Bria. I moved out here a few years ago when Barndel Accounting was hiring.

Rose: *Hurry up!*
Me: *I'm coming down now.*
Rose: *All the single men will be gone.*
Me: *We should focus on having fun, not getting laid.*
Rose: *That's your goal.*

When the elevator doors closed, I put my phone away and hit the lobby button. I released a breath and watched the numbers drop. When it dinged for me to step forward, I walked through the lobby and waved at Emmet, our security guard.

"You going out of town?" Emmet questioned as he held the door open for me.

I waved at Rose. "Just a little boat ride with my friends." Our weekends weren't synced up, but we made it a point to get together today.

She popped open the trunk and I jogged over to the car

to drop my bag inside. I opened the passenger side door, climbed in, and tossed my purse in the backseat.

"Baby, the weekend has begun!" Rose yelled, slapping hands with me.

I pulled out my shades and covered my eyes. "What time does the boat leave the dock?"

Rose glanced at the clock on the radio. "We have fifteen minutes to get there." Rose sped away and stopped at the end of the street, then hit the turn signal and sped into traffic. I lived a few hours from the beach in Seaside, so it was best that we left from my area of the city in Pleasantville. I popped a piece of gum and motioned to Rose. She declined, so I popped a piece in my mouth, turned up the music, and snapped my fingers to the beat of Halle's new song, dancing in my seat.

"I like the shorts," Rose pointed out. They showed off my long legs, curves, and wide hips.

"I just got this set the other day at Macy's."

Rose blew a kiss and giggled. "You look just as cute with your see-through dress."

We met through a mutual friend Bria Dawson when my firm needed a lawyer to go over documents in a lawsuit from a former client. Rose, being that lawyer, came highly recommended by Bria. Rose was a little taller at five-eight, with sepia-brown skin and reddish undertones. I loved her long braids and had thought about getting my hair done in knotless braids or dreads.

Recently, I had it cut short like Halle Berry in the earlier years of her career because it was easier to manage without much maintenance.

We pulled up to the dock and Rose found a spot near the front, pulling into the reserved space. I gestured to the *Reserved* sign. "What if we get a ticket?"

Rose shrugged and pulled her shades down from her head. "I know the owner of the boat." Rose popped the trunk and opened the door.

I climbed out to grab my things and followed her to the gate as people went to load up and leave. "Which boat are we going on?"

"Barry didn't say. It's called Lucy though."

I scanned the boats lined up to find the name, and my eyes widened in surprise. I tapped Rose on the shoulder and pointed at the massive yacht trimmed in gold. "Is that it?" I asked.

Rose looked at her phone and then back up. "The name says Lucy."

I fanned myself and tossed my bag over my shoulder. "Wow."

"I know. I thought it was a regular boat."

Rose as a lawyer by day was spot on, but when she was in date mode she threw all common sense out the window to get a man.

"We could live on that thing."

The guard waved for us to move forward. "What's your name?" he asked.

Rose held up the phone. "Rose, and this is Chanel."

He scanned the list of names and nodded. "You're good to go through." He wrapped a wristband on us.

We thanked him at the same time.

Rose linked her arm in mine. "I need the biggest margarita." She clung to me and laughed.

"Remember, no more than two drinks and water before we leave." The memory of the last time we went out together and I had to get the bodyguard from the club to help carry her out lingered.

Rose rolled her eyes. "Okay, Mom."

"I want to have fun, but let's not go crazy."

The music blasted off the yacht as shirtless men walked around with six and eight-pack muscles making me regret my decisions.

"Which one do you want?" Rose asked.

"Hell, I don't want to choose." Each one could make me impulsive, and I hated to lose control.

Rose stepped on the yacht. "Good, because it's our weekend, and we can be free to enjoy ourselves."

I followed her to the front deck near the DJ booth and smiled at the couple dancing with their arms around each other. "Bria!" I screamed and ran up to her and Cairo.

Bria pulled back. "Chanel! You finally made it!" Bria pointed at my clothes. "You look cute. I love this outfit." The woman was sophisticated, subtle, and sexy.

"Please, you're the one who's causing every head to turn."

Cairo's eyes narrowed at the men laughing in the corner. "Whose head?"

Bria chortled and dropped her hands from my waist. "Babe, stop being grouchy."

I loved their relationship.

Rose approached, drinking a margarita, and handed one to me. "We thought this was going to be a small boat."

"I knew you'd find the bar before anything else." Bria laughed and shook her head.

Rose nudged me in the arm. "Momma bear over here gave me a limit."

I sipped on the strawberry frozen sensation and shimmied my hips in happiness. I peered around the crowd, and it was a mixture of people I'd met before from Bria's job as a prosecutor and guys Cairo worked with.

"So, this is the big announcement celebration, correct?"

"Something like that. But let me show you guys the room you can freshen up in." Bria fell in step with us and we headed below deck.

"Cairo, I need you to tell me how many single men are here," Rose probed.

"Bria, call me when you're ready, babe. I'm going to hang with the guys." Cairo kissed her on the cheek and left us alone.

I rocked my hip toward her and booty bumped her. "You're so cute together."

"He's the best," Bria responded and opened the door of the suite we'd be staying in for the trip.

My mouth dropped in shock.

Rose jumped in excitement. "Wow, this is gorgeous."

"You didn't have to give us this large of a room, Bria," I said.

Bria reached for my bag and placed it near the closet. "Yes, I did. You deserve a trip away with friends."

Her hair flew out in silky tangles. "You two have everything you need, and room service is available," Bria said.

Rose looked around the large suite in awe. "I don't think I want to leave."

It was decorated in gold and black trimming. There were two large beds, a bathroom, vanity mirror, and walk-in closet.

"For right now, relax and freshen up," Bria said.

Rose dropped her bags near the end of the bed. "I'm ready to mix and mingle."

"Of course you are." I chuckled.

"We have food ready to eat, then you can meet the rest of the guests at the party."

"That's fine with me." The sheer logic of the amount of

money that went into this luxury yacht made me wish I had a different job.

Rose twisted her hips and poked out her tongue. "Then let's go party, ladies."

We left the room and made our way back through the crowd when I saw more people step on the boat. Cairo laughed at something one guy said.

I poked Bria in her arm. "Who is that talking to Cairo?"

She looked at the men. "That's Maddux, Cairo's team member."

Rose lifted her drink to her mouth and sipped. "He's staring at you, Chanel." She winked at me.

I held a hand over my eyes to cut out the sun. "Please, he's probably tried to get at every girl in here."

Rose pushed me forward. "The only one that has his attention from across the room is you."

I almost tripped. "Stop pushing me," I fussed and flipped her off.

Maddux was just what I needed to help get my mind off work and relax. He was taller than me with a short fade, muscular build, and a dark-mahogany skin tone.

"Maddux, when did you get here?" Bria asked.

Maddux wrapped an arm around Bria's neck. "Bria, you know Cairo waits until the last minute to tell me these things," Maddux joked.

"He is last minute with things," Bria teased, gripping Cairo's left hand.

Maddux dropped his arm as he licked his lips. "Who's your friend, Bria?" Maddux asked, rubbing his beard.

"Chanel, and she's available," Rose blurted out.

I choked on my drink, then clapped a hand on my chest to catch my breath.

Rose tapped me on my back.

"You good?" Maddux questioned, placing his hand on my lower back.

I glared at Rose. "I'm fine, thank you." My mind wanted to curse her out, but we were currently in front of new people so I needed to be cool and calm.

"Maddux works with Cairo," Bria said.

Rose tilted her head. "So, a military man?"

Maddux grinned and finished his beer. "Something like that." He placed the empty bottle in the trash.

"Looks like you all have coupled up, so I'm going to find someone to link with," Rose explained, then turned and walked off.

I shook my head. "I need a refill."

"I'll go with you," Bria said and headed to the bar with me.

We walked over and situated ourselves close to the stairs. Bria popped a few peanuts in her mouth.

I passed my empty glass to the bartender. "Can I get a refill please?" I adjusted with my back to the bar, and watched the crowd laugh and dance.

Bria bumped me with her shoulder. "He's watching you."

I turned my head in her direction. "Who?"

"Maddux."

I brushed the hair behind my ear. "He's cute."

"Single."

I shook my head. "I wonder how many women he's watched today."

Horn!

The loud noise of the DJ getting the crowd ramped up caused cheers and hands to rise in the air. Bria snapped her fingers, moved her hips, and joined in as the bartender handed me another drink. "Thanks."

I took a sip and moved to the middle of the boat. I danced with Bria and a few other people. Closing my eyes, I let the alcohol seep through me. A hard chest came up behind me, and slowly, I moved my hips to the beat. When he caught the rhythm, he followed my motions.

His lips grazed against my ear. "I admire your moves."

I felt reckless. I whipped around to face him and wrapped my left arm around his shoulder. "Thanks, you're not bad yourself."

He pulled me in closer. "You want to go somewhere and talk?"

The boat had filled with more people that I hadn't seen when I first stepped on. I finished the drink and moved back for him to lead the way.

"How long have you been here?" I placed my empty glass down on the bar, and Maddux grasped my hand as we sauntered to the lower deck.

"Not that long. Like I said, Cairo was last minute with the invite."

We entered the dining room, which wasn't as crowded as upstairs, and took a seat near the television and fireplace.

"What about you?" Maddux put his beer down on the side table next to the seat.

I crossed my legs, facing him. "Same as you. My weekend getaway." I held both index and middle finger up as air quotes.

Maddux scrubbed his chin. "Workaholic?"

"Yes. Don't get me wrong, I like my job, but sometimes it can be stressful."

"What do you do?"

"Accountant."

Maddux clasped his hands together and sat back. "Math was my worst subject in school." He chuckled.

"I love math and history. It's not that bad." I laid my head against the back of the seat.

Maddux caressed my cheek. "I will let you be the expert, Miss Lady."

"Call me Chanel."

"All right, Chanel. So, what's the deal with you and a boyfriend?"

"I don't have a boyfriend."

"Good, but I wouldn't have cared if you had one."

I cackled. "Why is that?"

Maddux shrugged, looping our hands together. "He's not me."

I pretended to get up. "See, you're too cocky for me."

He nudged me back down. Only this time, I landed in his lap. He chuckled, and I allowed his large, warm hands to keep me in place.

I faced him and crossed my leg, pulling my shorts down a little. "Bria left that part out."

"Bria's a cool chick. She's become like a little sister to the guys."

I pointed at the seat next to us. "Can I sit down on my own, or do I have to stay in your lap?"

Maddux shook his head. "No, I like you in my space."

I raised a brow. "You don't know me."

"Yet."

"Huh?"

As bad as I wanted to kiss his perfect lips, I had to keep my horniness under control.

"I don't know you *yet*." This man was aware of his power and how women fell at his feet.

"What if your girlfriend tries to fight me?" I am the friend who would tell my girls to never fight over a man, but Maddux was a different story.

His brow furrowed. "No girlfriend."

I reared back in confusion. "Wife?"

Maddux counted on his fingers. "No wife, fiancée, booty call, or nothing."

We both burst into laughter at his comment, and I slid off his lap.

He lifted my legs and placed them over the couch. "I like your laugh."

"You're determined to keep me close." At first I might have been hesitant, but Maddux had been nothing but a gentleman with charm.

"A part of my master plan."

I wagged a finger in his face. "I need to keep my eye on you, Maddux."

Maddux raised both hands in surrender. "Please do, because I'm doing the same."

"How old are you?"

Even the air seemed to be holding in its breath. The waves were steady and calm, and guests walked around us without interrupting.

"Thirty-two, one of the youngest of the group."

"I'm thirty."

Once again he caressed my cheek. "Sexy, funny, and smart."

"For such a big guy, you have soft hands." A shiver ran through my body, and I prayed it wasn't obvious how much his touch drove me crazy.

"Some people would say I'm like a big teddy bear, but I can kick ass if you need me to."

I blew out a breath. "I wish you were around with my old boyfriends."

The elegance of the interior became my safety net as a distraction from his sexiness.

"Naw, you wouldn't have even met them if I knew you back then."

The door of the dining room opened, and Bria poked her head in and grinned. "I wanted to check up on you."

"Did we miss the announcement?" I asked, sliding to get up.

Bria motioned for me to stay seated. "No, you're fine. We have time."

"Okay, great. Maddux was just filling me in on how funny and smart I am."

He cupped my chin. "And sexy," he added.

I covered my face in embarrassment.

"Maddux is a charmer. I see you, girl," Bria teased, waving her finger at him.

"Where's Rose?"

Bria pointed to the back deck. "She's found a prospective date, so I left her alone." Bria giggled.

I rolled my eyes, looking through the window. "Maybe I should go check on her."

"No, she's fine. Besides, Maddux looks like he'll be lost if you leave him." Bria pointed at him.

I turned my head to look.

Maddux poked out his bottom lip in a pout. "Miss Lady, don't break my heart."

I playfully slapped him on his chest, and our hands joined together automatically.

Maddux smirked, causing my heart to beat faster.

"I will leave you two alone." Bria turned and walked out.

"Tell me something about yourself," I asked, enjoying the time we'd spent together. Maddux bit his bottom lip. "I like to read."

His response surprised me. "Really? Like what?"

"Man, don't tell anybody, Miss Lady."

I folded my arms together and cocked my head to the side. "I won't. Why do you keep calling me Miss Lady?"

He shrugged, running his tongue over the top of his teeth. "You seem classy and sweet, but you're not ready for me, baby." Maddux smirked.

"We won't even see each other after today, so to give me a nickname is a little arrogant, don't you think?"

Maddux wrapped his finger around a strand of my hair. The tenderness in his eyes wanted to combat my statement. "Tell me something about you?"

"I'm a terrible driver."

"That's your answer."

"What? I can't give all my secrets away."

Maddux backed up and spread his legs wide, the jeans showing his long, wide thighs. "You're trouble, Miss Lady."

"Good trouble."

The door flew open, and Rose stomped in with her shirt soaking wet.

I jumped up to help. "What happened?"

She reached for some napkins. "Some waitress spilled crab sauce all over me!" Rose cried.

I stared at him with hope. "Let me help you. Maddux, do you mind if we finish this conversation later?"

Maddux stood and kissed me on the forehead. "It's cool. Take care of your friend."

I smiled, grasped Rose's hand, and helped her to our room. Earlier she walked in proud and ready to party it up. Now I wondered if she'd want to leave immediately and cause me to lose out on more time with Maddux.

Chapter 2

Chanel

Rose slammed the door behind her, slid her shorts down, and tossed them on the floor.

"Sorry, you had to leave your boyfriend."

I grabbed her bag. "He's not my boyfriend," I said as I tossed her a bra and dress.

"Ugh, before the food spill, I met this guy Lamont." Rose went into the bathroom and turned on the shower.

I sat on the edge of the bed and peered at the door. "Use protection."

Fifteen minutes later, the water turned off.

Rose stepped out with a towel wrapped around her body. "I wasn't planning on dipping out." She sat near the bed and picked up her lotion.

I waved off her words. "You're grown. Do you."

Knock! Knock!

I jumped up and went to open the door.

"You guys okay?" Bria asked.

Rose released the towel after she had on her underwear. "The waitress dropped food on me. I needed to change." Rose checked herself out in the mirror.

Bria moved in closer. "Sorry about that."

"It's not your fault." As usual Rose piled on makeup, ready to get back in the saddle.

Bria planted a hand on her hip. "Are you guys ready to eat?"

"Yes," we answered at the same time.

Bria treaded out of the room with the door gently open. "The announcement is happening, and the food is being served."

Rose linked her arm in mine as we headed back out to mingle. People were still dancing on the upper deck and drinking, while some were in the dining room. I glanced around and saw Maddux talking to Cairo.

"No seating arrangement," Bria announced.

Rose released my arm and walked over to a guy who was talking to another woman. I guess that was Lamont because she whispered in the girl's ear, and she tossed her napkin on the table and moved to another seat.

"He's going to have problems with her," Bria mumbled.

I laughed and walked around the table to take a seat. A chair was pulled out, and I smiled as Maddux stood and waited for me to sit down like a gentleman. "You saved me a seat." I picked up the napkin and placed it on my lap.

"I like having your company."

"I agree." It felt like high school again with the jock being interested in me.

Bria sat next to Cairo and gripped her glass of water. "We have an announcement to make. The reason you've been invited here." Bria smiled at Cairo.

He slid his hand to her palm.

"I'm pregnant!" Bria shouted.

The entire room lit up in excitement.

I stood up and went to hug her, then Cairo shook hands with the guys.

"Glad I didn't have to hold that in any longer," Cairo joked, slapping hands with a few of the guys at the table.

"You know what you're having?" another guest asked.

Bria rubbed her belly. "We want to be surprised."

The staff came around to serve food and refill glasses as everyone fell into conversation with the person next to them or across the table.

"Imagine if Cairo has a daughter," I teased.

"I can hear Aydin now trying to calm me down," Cairo replied.

Bria cupped Cairo's cheek and pecked him on the lips, then wiped away her lipstick. "I just want a healthy baby," Bria answered.

I looped my arm around her shoulder and squeezed her tight in comfort. "I'm so happy for you and Cairo," I said, then sat back down next to Maddux.

Cairo held his glass up in the air to give a toast. "Time to eat and then continue the party."

Everybody clinked glasses in acknowledgement.

Staff placed an array of foods, including lobster, steak, chicken, and pasta, in front of us. Only thing we could hear was either Bria answering questions on her pregnancy or utensils preparing to cut into the lobster and pasta.

"Any plans afterwards?" Maddux questioned.

I motioned to the front of the boat. "Sit out on the deck."

Maddux laid his arm on the back of my chair. "So, I can get more of your time?"

I sat back with my head against his arm. "Depends."

He peered at my lips. "On what?"

I slid a piece of fish in my mouth. "What do you have in

mind?" A little sauce dripped down my lip and I went to wipe it off when he stopped me.

Maddux smirked, then lifted his finger to gently run across my lip and chin. I couldn't say the last time I had a connection like this.

* * *

The creak of the bed as he laid me down was the only sound in the room. He slid off my cover-up and threw it on the ground, then leaned over me and caressed my cheek. Our eyes connected, and my entire body became hot from his touch as he grazed a hand across my thigh. His smooth skin against my body brought chills. I'd never had a one-night stand and threw caution to the wind. Maddux slid his tongue up my arm, across my shoulder, and to my throat. Curious, I ran a hand over the curly hairs on his upper chest, down to his abdomen, and then to his thickness. I sucked in a gasp when he trailed his lips down my chest and gently sucked my left nipple.

"Miss Lady," he groaned as his hand slid across my belly.

"Hmmm... Maddux." I moaned, clasping the sheets in my hand.

He stopped nibbling on my breast. "Are you sure about what's to come?"

I stared at him. "I'm positive." It was my own driving need that shocked me.

"You ready for me to fuck you, Miss Lady?"

"Yes, I'm ready." My thoughts spun as shivers of delight followed his touch.

"Good answer."

Maddux blew air across my left nipple, then right, and

slowly massaged them. The gentle massage sent currents of desire through me. All I wanted was for him to stop torturing me and take me to the edge.

"Maddux!"

"Ssshh. I'm running things."

Maddux took control, leaned up, slid his tongue over my lips, and nudged my mouth open. I groaned as his tongue swirled in my mouth. I reached down between our joined bodies and squeezed his dick. He pulled back, and I pouted as I watched him pull out his wallet and grab a condom. I removed the rest of my bikini, and Maddux took off his shorts. He slid the condom on and bent over again to brush his lips along my jawline and cheek. I spread my legs wider as he pressed inside me.

I arched off the bed. "Ughh..."

"Shit, Miss Lady!" Maddux mumbled as his body imprisoned mine in a web of growing arousal.

I tossed a hand against the headboard as he thrust forward, then moaned in his ear. His large body engulfed the entire bed, and I hoped nobody heard us. My small hands went to both sides of his face and pressed kisses across his cheeks, chin, and lips. He broke away and grasped both breasts and flicked his tongue while he squeezed and pumped faster.

"Sexy as fuck, Miss Lady."

"Maddux, please," I pleaded, as my chest heaved up and down.

His thick hardness and heavy balls had the bed shaking, while our voices could probably be heard over the music. We hadn't even waited until the meal was over before we came back to his room. My mouth opened, then closed on an unintelligible gasp.

Maddux's head flew back as he rocked in and out. "This is perfect," he groaned.

I was sweaty and overheated, and I could feel my orgasm approaching quickly. I'd never had this experience with any other guy before.

"Ohhh... Maddux!"

His grip tightened on my ass cheeks. I couldn't hold on any longer and finally let go.

"Fuck! Chanel, right there, beautiful." His eyes drew into slits, and his mouth opened as he came right behind me.

This was the most excitement I'd had in years, and I was ready for more. Maddux pulled out of me and walked to the bathroom as I curled up in the sheets. A few minutes later, I felt a kiss on my forehead.

"Thank you, Miss Lady."

I smiled and nodded as my eyes dipped low into a long sleep.

* * *

Hours later, I felt someone nudge me awake, and I yawned, stretching out my arms. Rose stood in front of me with a smirk on her face.

She tapped me on the shoulder. "Wake up, Lolita."

I slowly opened my eyes. Still in a haze, I looked out the window. It was dark out.

Checking my watch, I saw it was close to seven at night. "What happened?" I scanned the room to get my thoughts together.

"You don't remember?"

I placed a hand on my forehead, closed my eyes, and grinned.

Rose tittered, then bent down and picked up the bikini top. "I know what that grin is for."

I snatched the top from her hands. "Shut up." When I sat up in bed and started to get out, I remembered I was naked.

"How was it?"

"What?"

Rose climbed on the bed next to me. "Maddux, girl."

She tried to lift the covers, but I smacked her hand away. "What are you talking about?"

"Girl, I heard you two."

I gasped, covered my mouth, and giggled. "Shut up. No, you didn't."

Rose turned to face me. "I did, and he came back up to the deck all smiling."

I covered my face in shame. "Please tell me you didn't say anything to him."

"I just asked if you were still alive after all that howling," Rose teased.

I lifted a pillow to throw at her. "I was not howling."

"Ugh! Yes, Maddux! Please!" Rose reenacted, using a pillow.

"Shut up!" I laughed.

Rose tossed the pillow on the ground. "He said to let you rest."

I pulled the sheet around my body and climbed out of the bed. "I'm not talking about this with you." I grabbed clothes from the suitcase then went to the bathroom.

Rose sat up on the bed and scrolled her phone. "Glad one of us had a little fun."

I poked my head out with a toothbrush in my mouth. "What about Lamont?"

Rose waved me off. "He's engaged."

My eyebrows rose in shock. "He lied!"

Rose shrugged. "Glad I found out now. Anyway, we're headed back home, so get dressed."

"All right. Have Bria and Cairo already left?"

Rose got off the bed and stretched her arms. "They're telling people goodbye now."

"I will wash up real quick, and then we can leave."

She stood at the door. "That's fine. Did you have fun overall?"

I turned off the faucet and finished cleaning myself. "It was fun. We have to come back."

"That's cool. Maybe we'll do something on our own when we get back home." She shrugged.

"Like what?"

"Maybe a dating cruise."

I got dressed and walked out of the bathroom, tossing the sheets in the corner of the room. "That doesn't appeal to me, Rose."

Rose helped me grab my bags. "It can be for me, since you've met your future husband."

I slid my feet in my shoes. "It was a one-night stand. Nothing more."

We sauntered to the upper deck to see Bria and Cairo as they waved goodbye to their guests. I gazed around to see if Maddux was still around.

Rose tapped me on the shoulder. "He's gone."

"What?"

"Your lover left already," Rose taunted, poking me in the arm.

"I was not thinking about him."

She rolled her eyes. "Yeah, sure you weren't."

I reached out to hug Cairo and then Bria. "Bria, Cairo, thank you again for the trip. We had a good time."

Bria looked up at Cairo. "Baby, can I talk to them privately?"

"Sure. It was good to see you two again." He pointed at the staff, then walked over to the bartender to help clean up.

"Spill it," Bria said.

I dropped my bag on the floor to search my purse and grab my cell. "Spill what?"

Bria gleefully clapped her hands together. "Rose said you had sex with Maddux."

"Rooooseeee," I whined and released a breath, glad most of the guests were gone and not here to witness my nervousness.

"She promised I could be the godmother," Rose joked.

I flipped her off. "It didn't mean anything, just two people having a good time."

Bria lifted her fingers and pretended to zip her lips. "No judgement over here."

"Thanks, Bria."

"Remember to call me when you two make it home." Bria hugged us both again, then trekked to the bar to meet Cairo.

Rose waved goodbye and I trailed beside her. We stepped off the boat and walked to the car. We tossed our bags inside and jumped in.

She turned down the radio, and asked, "Did you get his number?"

I peeled a piece of gum from my pocket. "No." A pain squeezed my heart as I thought of him.

"Do you know his last name?"

"No." My stomach dropped at forgetting to even get his last name.

She held her hand out for a high five. "That's my girl!"

I pushed her hand down. "You're proud of my whorish behavior?"

"All women get one night to let loose."

She placed the car in reverse, backed out, and drove to the city.

I leaned my head on the back of the seat and closed my eyes in remembrance of his soft touch.

* * *

A few weeks later

I ran into my office, dropped my purse and briefcase on the desk, and picked up the phone.

"Hello, Chanel Forrest." I turned on the computer, pushed the phone between my shoulder and ear, and typed in my password. The door opened, and Moria, the other accountant, approached my desk with a file folder.

"Chanel, it's Roland. I wanted to see if you have time to run through our accounts."

The owner of Roland Simpson Construction and Real Estate was a longtime client of the company.

"Thanks, Moria. Uhm, Roland, did you have anything specific you wanted to discuss?"

I flipped through the file folder and saw it was the latest numbers for the law firm who'd just signed a contract for our services.

"My team is planning a new bid on a location, and I want to get your ideas," Roland explained.

I slumped down in the chair. "Can you send me the preliminary numbers?"

"I can email them over."

"Thanks, Roland. I will contact you once I look over everything."

We hung up, and I sat back in my chair, blowing out a frustrated breath. Over the last few weeks, I had been working overtime, plus going out with Rose, and spending every little moment thinking about Maddux. It bothered me that I never got his last name, even though it was a one-time thing.

"What did he want?" Moria still stood at the door of my office.

I grabbed the mouse and opened my email. "He's sending over a bid for a new project." I looked to see if he'd sent it yet, then looked through the files on my desk.

Moria stepped up to my desk. "Ohh, maybe this will bring a big bonus."

I removed my jacket and unbuttoned the wrists of my shirt. "Hopefully." I signed into the quarterly numbers of each client I oversaw, and my brows dipped low in confusion. I tapped my nails on the desk.

Moria crossed her arms. "You seem distracted."

I leaned in closer to the screen. "Did anyone work on my accounts while I was gone?"

She came around to look at my computer. "Not that I know of. Why?"

"Hmmm... Strange to see that two of my accounts have dropped off."

"What do you mean?" Moria stood behind me and leaned into the screen.

I pointed at the two accounts that I had managed for the past year. "Roland and Nature's Fine Fabrics isn't showing up." I searched the database of the company to pull up information that everyone had access to see.

Moria gestured at the screen. "This shows that Darlene was last logged in two days ago."

I reared back and frowned. "Why is she looking at my accounts?"

"Good question."

Knock! Knock!

"Meeting in the conference room," Joey, the supervising accountant in our department, said.

I grabbed my pen and notebook. Lately, my numbers were growing, and everyone saw how I was the accountant who brought in the most clients. If he went behind my back and put my rival in charge, that meant he was more than likely sleeping with her because Joey didn't do anything nice for anyone.

Chapter 3

Maddux

I tossed the basketball toward the basket, and Cairo slapped it down. I threw my hands in the air, pissed off that Bishop and I were losing to him, Jasper, and Soaquan.

"Turnover!" I yelled, and they both laughed at me.

"Give it up, Maddux. You're losing," Soaquan taunted me.

I held my hands out for the ball. It's not over until we hit twenty-one." I pointed at the screen on the back of the board showing Bishop and me down by three points. Cairo drove out here with Bria after the party a few weeks ago. We'd just gotten back from a mission recently and decided to play a round of ball at the local center to hang out.

"Fine, let's see if you can get it in the hole this time."

"That's what she said!" I joked and passed the ball to Bishop, who took a shot. Soaquan and Cairo stood surprised as they watched the ball fall in the basket.

"Down by one," Bishop said.

"Time." Soaquan held his hand up in a T-shape.

I busted out in laughter at him cheating. "You can't call timeout."

The door opened, and we turned to see Aydin march inside with a scowl on his face.

"Aydin, what's up?" Cairo questioned.

He gripped a folder in his hand. "We got a case."

I held the ball up. "Talk to us."

I searched Aydin's face. Something was off about this case already.

"Victor sent over a file on some pirates." Aydin rarely came out here from Memphis unless it was a major issue. His team and ours communicated back and forth if one group couldn't take on a large caseload.

"Pirates?" I chuckled, and they stared at me.

Cairo nudged me in the arm. "Ignore him."

Aydin held the file out to Cairo, and he opened it.

"Not exactly pirates, but gun smugglers that run as a biker crew. I know Cairo is technically taking some time off, so I think Maddux should take the lead," Aydin explained.

I grinned, rubbing my hands together. I was known as the little brother of the group. They didn't take me seriously, but everybody knew I was a straight shooter when it came to catching suspects. I grew up in Clarksville as the son of a veteran. I'd lived all over the country and internationally, from England to Japan, because of my dad's career. I learned from the best and joined the Navy. I got to do what I loved, from protecting my country, to traveling the world, to meeting different women. Micah and Maise Hayes were retired now and on me about settling down, but I kept reminding them it wasn't in my blood to settle down with a woman and get married.

Jasper came over and grabbed a towel off the bench. "You're going to put Maddux in charge?"

Aydin slipped his cell out of his pocket. "He's going to have me alongside, but he will take the lead."

Cairo handed the file to me.

As I scanned over the notes and photos, I saw it was a group of men with rifles and shotguns in ski masks aboard three different boats. People like this pissed me off because they thought they were invincible.

"What are you thinking?" Cairo questioned, stood next to me.

I flipped to the next photo of the scene. "Has Columbo looked into the last known locations they've shown up?"

Everyone waited on Aydin's response.

"He is sending the information over as we speak. Check your email." Aydin read a message from Columbo, our tech guy.

Cairo gave a look of worry. "You think you can handle this?" The need to be out in the field could be seen in his eyes. With Bria early in her pregnancy I knew he wanted to be close to her at this time.

"I know I can handle this. Who's the leader?"

"Based on photo recognition in the FBI and Interpol database, Rayo Cavente and his boys are a part of a smuggling gang," Cairo said, then flipped over the next photo.

"Damn," I swore, staring at photos of piles of money, guns, and jewelry.

Aydin brushed a hand down his face. "Yeah, they've stolen up to forty million in money, jewels, and then used some of that to run guns through the country."

"If they have that much accumulated, you'd think it would be time to stop," Soaquan remarked.

"Once people get a taste of that lifestyle, there's no turning back," Cairo said.

I nodded, then handed the file to Soaquan. "I want to get more information from Columbo before we fly out."

Aydin clapped me on the shoulder and extended his hand for a shake. "I agree. Let's relax for tonight. Tomorrow, we meet at the office."

"Are you heading home?" Cairo asked.

I lifted my gym bag and placed it on my shoulder. "I need to shower and run by my folks' place. Then I'm free."

"Tell Pops we still need to get that fishing trip together."

I shook hands with the guys as we left the center. "Better you than me. I hate getting up at five in the morning."

Soaquan popped me on the back of the head. "We do that for missions." He trailed alongside me out of the building.

I pulled my keys out of my pocket and hit the button to unlock my Jeep Wrangler. "That's different," I mentioned.

Soaquan threw his bag in the back of his jeep. "How?"

I slid one leg inside my driver's side. "I like catching the bad guys. It gives me a rush. To leave my warm bed for smelly fish is not my idea of fun."

* * *

Twenty minutes later, I knocked on my parents' door, pushed it open, and walked in as their dog ran at me.

"Micah Jr., you've been a good boy." I rubbed the top of his head, and he rolled over on his stomach. We'd had Micah Jr. since I was a little kid when my dad brought him home to cheer me up because we had to move out of Clarksville and permanently make Nashville our home base. He was a golden retriever, protective of the family, and spoiled. I heard a throat clear and looked up to see my mom standing with her arms crossed and a towel on her shoulder.

"Now you look too pretty to have your face scrunched up." I walked up to her and held my arms out for a hug.

She hit me with the towel and hugged me. "Sweet talking me won't get you anywhere."

I kissed her on the cheek and forehead. "Would my undying love help?" I pulled back and smiled.

"Maybe." She laughed and turned to head to the kitchen.

I followed and saw Dad reading the paper. This was a normal thing for them whenever she was in the kitchen. He needed to be near her. When he is out cutting the grass, she sat on the porch with a cold glass of lemonade. Those little things made me admire my parents and the love they'd been able to protect for all these years.

I peeked in the pot on the stove. "Where's Mykelti?"

"He has some big party for work," Mom explained, slapping my hand away.

I reminded myself to text my older brother about catching up when he got back into town. We were close, but our jobs were demanding, so the only time we saw each other was at family functions.

I grabbed a bottle of water from the fridge and propped up on the island in the middle of the kitchen. Mykelti and I had the idea to buy our parents a house to celebrate his retirement. My father refused at first, but after months of breaking him out of his stubborn shell, he okayed the two-story, ten-thousand-square-foot brick home that sat in a quiet cul de sac not too far from me.

I went to pick up a piece of shrimp. "When is he back?"

Slap!

Mom smacked my hand and pushed me away from the stove.

"Ouch!"

She wagged her finger at me. "Dinner is ready in five minutes."

Dad picked up his drink and closed the paper. "He said in a few days, depending on the case."

Mykelti worked as a manager for a high-end Wenton Hotel in East Nashville and recently got engaged to his girl-friend, an elementary school teacher named Lizzy.

"I have to hit him up so we can catch up."

"Go sit down and take this with you." Mom motioned for me to take the plate off the stove.

I jumped down off the island and grabbed the plate to set in the middle of the table. I removed my jacket, ready to dig into the platter of shrimp and wild rice. Mom took the seat next to Dad and filled her glass with wine.

"When are you going to meet a nice girl like your broth-er?" Mom smiled, then pushed my father in the arm at the shake of his head.

Mom lifted her fork to her mouth. "What's funny, Micah?"

"Leave that boy alone, Maise." Dad chuckled.

Mom ate more of her rice. "He needs to meet a good woman. Someone who can cook for him."

I stopped chewing and picked up the water bottle, ignoring her question. Mom was hellbent on marrying me to someone from her circle, but all her friends' daughters were too prissy. I smirked to myself at the memory of Chanel on the boat and the way she felt in my arms.

"What's that smile on your face?"

"I'm not smiling." I burped and piled more food on my plate.

Mom dropped her fork in excitement. "You met someone."

"Maise," Dad called out.

"No," I replied, ignoring her stare.

She held her hands up in the air in prayer. "Yes, you did." Then she clapped her hands in excitement while she danced in her seat.

I pointed my fork at her and gestured. "Get your wife, man."

Dad grumbled, cleaning the rest of his plate. "Let your mother have her excitement."

I shook my head and continued to eat as she glared at me. "Do you really want to hear about a one-night stand?"

"Maddux!" Mom wanted me to be like my brother and settle down and give her grandkids.

"What? I'm grown, and I met a woman. We hit it off, and then I came back home."

"In Pleasantville?" She's warm-hearted but pushy when she tries to parent me when I'm no longer a little boy.

"Yep," I answered.

"Did you get her number at least?" Nancy Drew continued with her questions.

I put more rice in my mouth. "Nope."

Mom reached her hand out and grabbed my mouth while I was still eating. "What's her name?"

I looked at Dad for help, and he ignored us both. "Chanel." I removed her hand.

"What does she do?"

"I don't know."

Mom laid her fork down, leaned forward, and counted

on her right hand. "You don't know where she works. There's no number. What's her last name?"

I froze and cursed under my breath for not getting shorty's last name. "Uhm...shit." I slouched in the chair.

Mom slapped me on the back of the head. "I didn't raise you to go around spreading your little penis to everybody," Mom complained.

"Ma!" I groaned, running a hand down my face.

"Maise, leave the boy alone. He's thirty-two," Dad said.

"I don't care if he's fifty. My son will not run around the world sleeping with women and not even knowing last names," she chastised as she snatched my plate away.

"If it makes you feel any better, she's friends with Cairo and Bria."

She pursed her lips in thought and handed the plate back to me. "Fine, at least she has good taste in friends. Can't say the same for the men she sleeps with." She rolled her eyes.

I held my hand to my chest in offense. "That hurts, old woman."

"Boy! Call me old woman again and see what happens." Her face collapsed into a complex set of wrinkles.

I chuckled and finished my meal. We talked and laughed about us being kids. Eventually, I helped her clean up, grabbed a beer out of the fridge, and sat on the porch with Pops.

Dad smoked on his pipe. "You almost gave your mom a heart attack."

The neighborhood was quiet around this time with most families indoors. They were a few younger kids, but mostly older couples and retired veterans lived amongst them. Sometimes, Mom would volunteer to babysit since me and my brother hadn't given her grandkids yet.

I lifted the bottle to my lips and gulped it down. "That woman is crazy."

He smiled and drank his beer. "Yeah, and I love every minute of her crazy." His features carried a sense of pride. Pops and I had the same features and build, he still worked out to this day at his age.

"Sometimes I wonder if I'll be with a woman like Mom."

"What do you mean?"

I propped my arm on the back of the seat. "Somebody strong who can handle my life and the work I do."

"If she loves you, she will."

"Hopefully. Most women don't like the distance."

He nodded in agreement and rubbed his beard. "True, but love is sacrifice and if you're willing to have that person a hundred percent, then you need to give a hundred and ten."

I drank the rest of the beer. "Enough about me. What are you up to besides listening to Mom boss you around," I joked.

He placed his pipe on the table, clasped his hands together, and stared at the yard. "She thinks she bosses me around. Retirement is peaceful, but I miss the action sometimes."

"I understand. We got a new case I'm leading."

He smiled, extending a hand for a shake. "They finally put you in charge?"

I tapped my chest and sat up straight. "Aydin is there, of course, but most of the decisions will come from me."

"What's the case?"

"Gun smugglers."

He whistled. "Be careful."

I checked my watch. "Always. We have a meeting in the

morning." I wondered if I would ever get to a point like Cairo and want to slow down in the field. "I need to be heading home to get some rest."

Dad stood and embraced me in a hug. "Drive safe and text me when you get home."

I passed him my empty beer bottle to trash, and we shook hands. "Thanks, Dad." I walked to my car and started the engine as he watched me leave.

* * *

The next morning, I parked my bike at the office and hopped off, removing my helmet. I stalked inside and dropped it on the desk, then slapped hands with Soaquan and Bishop. All the offices were open-concept and sat on one level with a conference room. The breakroom and gym were in the back. Cairo had the place redecorated by Bria after they got married. She had wanted to put a woman's touch on it so it wasn't so dark. The aroma of coffee with a hint of cinnamon hit my nose.

Soaquan pushed a cup of coffee in my hand. "You're late on your first day of leading a meeting." He liked to rip on everybody.

I sipped on the coffee and reached for the biker magazine he was looking at. "Long night."

"After your basketball skills, I doubt it was long," Soaquan teased.

I flipped him off, trekked to my office, and took the file on the Cavente gang from my bag. "Is Aydin here?" I asked.

Bishop snatched the magazine back. "Yep, he's waiting for you to get here."

Soaquan stood at my door. "What are your thoughts?"

Bishop propped his legs up on his desk and threw a ball in the air.

"From reading over the FBI files, they've been watching the Cavente gang for a while." I studied the photos of each man. All wore a leather jacket with the Cavente logo and each man had tattoos across their knuckles.

"Columbo should be sending over the coordinates now," Soaquan informed me as he moved closer and picked up a few photos from the folder.

Aydin popped in with Nasir and Jasper. "Let's meet."

I jumped up and followed him to the conference room with my notes and the photos. Aydin opened the door, headed to the front of the table, and then turned on the computer monitor.

"What do you got?" Aydin questioned.

I tossed the photos on the table, took the remote to the computer, and scanned through the images. "So far, we know Rayo doesn't hit the same location twice."

"Tell us something we don't know," Nasir joked.

I shot a look at him. "Checking the timeline from the last three hits they've done, another is coming in a few weeks."

Everyone stared at each other, then at me.

"Are you sure?" Cairo asked.

I pointed at the timeline I sequenced on the screen. "Look at the patterns. They've robbed someone every three months. I give them credit for consistency, but mistakes show."

The next slide showed Rayo talking with a familiar enemy of Cairo's who we took down. Moses Giovanni had a Glock in his hands, surrounded by Rayo and his crew purchasing crates of guns.

Aydin balled up his fists and leaned against the table.

"Moses Giovanni." Aydin slammed the top of the table in frustration.

"Seriously!" Soaquan blurted his mouth dropping open in shock.

"Same thing I said." Moses wrapped in this bullshit with Rayo would only put us in a worse position.

Cairo ambled up to the front of the screen and pointed. "When was this taken?"

"At least a year ago based on the timestamp."

Cairo stared at the screen.

Aydin paced back and forth, and Nasir spoke to calm him down.

"What are you thinking?" I asked.

"We took down Moses, but I wonder if Rayo and his crew helped him," Aydin explained.

"How? If Rayo's had the feds following him this long, you'd think Moses would stay away from him," I challenged as I bent over the table and pushed the phone records toward him.

"I don't know. Moses had to have known we'd eventually catch his associates," Aydin commented.

"Get Columbo to send over everything he has," Cairo said.

I finished my text to Columbo then faced the team. "Waiting on Columbo to email over the documents now."

"Cairo, what is Bria saying about Moses?" Soaquan questioned.

"Nothing. She still has nightmares every once in a while, but we've been good."

"Can we get her to send over any contacts she has from her case on Moses?" I asked.

Cairo sat back in his chair and ran a hand over his head

in frustration. "She's pregnant now. I'd rather she stay away from this mess."

"Maybe we can have her office send the documents to us?" I knew Bria was his world and not having her in danger was his number one priority.

Flying back to New York was a last-minute thought, but we needed to cover every detail and find out if our contacts in the DEA or FBI could provide more information on their end.

Chapter 4

Chanel

I felt nauseous suddenly.

David, another employee, stepped into my office eating a cheese, egg, and sardines sandwich. "You okay?" He had no clue what the smell was doing to me. "Morning, brats." David bit into his sandwich.

I was ready to throw up. "I...I...need to use the restroom." I jumped up and ran out of my office. Brushing by another coworker, I pushed open the stall and threw up the oatmeal and bacon I had this morning. Once my stomach calmed down I wiped my mouth and walked to the sink to wash my hands. The door opened, and Moria looked at me with furrowed brows, her mouth thinned.

She snatched the paper towel from the holder and passed it to me. "Are you okay?"

I wiped my mouth and dried my hands. "Yeah, it was probably food poisoning."

Moria stood next to the counter, brow hiked. "Food poisoning?"

"Why are you looking at me like that?" I frowned.

She huffed, grabbed more paper towels and wet them

before handing them to me. "You seem flushed, and the other day, you ate all of my fries at lunch."

I walked out and headed to my office. "What are you talking about?"

She followed me and took a seat at my desk. "Just a thought but maybe take a pregnancy test." The light suddenly shined over the ceiling and gave me a piercing headache.

I opened my lunch box and grabbed a bottle of water, then sat in my chair. "No."

"Why not?" she wondered.

I flicked the keys on my computer to read over the latest data. "Because I'm not pregnant." I checked my email and saw that Roland had sent over his contract information.

She squinted with a pout. "How do you know?" Moria loved to be in everyone's business.

I forwarded it to my personal email and decided to work from home. "I haven't had sex." I closed the folder, logged out of my computer, and grabbed my jacket and purse.

"What about the boat party?" Moria probed.

I froze, closed my eyes, and cursed under my breath. "Oh my God, fuck." I had been different for once in my life and if the consequences caused a baby, I would only have myself to blame.

Moria's eyes narrowed at me in pity. "Please tell me you used protection."

"I need to get a test." The very thought of being someone's mom from a one-night stand never crossed my mind.

"Are you okay to drive?"

I nodded and pulled my keys out of my bag. "Can you take my meetings?"

Moria agreed and rubbed a hand down my arm. "Yeah, do you need me to call anyone?"

"No, I'll be fine. Just food poisoning." I was in denial.

She held up both hands and said, "Cross your fingers."

I pushed the button for the elevator and rubbed my temple nervously. The doors opened, and I stepped in then hit the lobby button. As the doors closed, my phone vibrated. I pulled it out of my purse to see a message from my father.

Dad: *Hey, sugar. Dinner tonight?*

I smiled as the elevator stopped at the lobby. I sauntered out of the building and sent a text back.

Me: *Hey, old man. Are we meeting at my favorite place?*
Dad: *I got your old man, little girl.*
Me: *lol! I'll be there for dinner.*

I closed the message thread and hopped in my car, tossing my things on the passenger seat. There was no way I could be pregnant. All my life, I'd been responsible and used protection with my sexual partners. If this was true, my father would kill me. Craig Forrest was a retired city worker, and he raised me after my mom passed away giving birth to me. He'd been a single dad all my life, dating on and off recently as far as I knew. I doubted he'd disown me, but I'd hate for him to be disappointed in his only child. Headed in the direction of the corner store near the restaurant, parked and rushed inside down the aisle and grabbed three tests just to be on the safe side. After paying I stuck them in my purse and drove to meet my father.

I parked at Melba's, a well-known restaurant that served the best home-cooked soul food. The hostess started to speak, and I pointed to my father sitting at the table near the window.

"Your waitress will be with you soon."

I waved at him and removed my jacket. "Thank you." Nerves still high, I tried to keep a neutral tone as I approached the table.

He stood to hug me, then took my jacket and placed it on the back of my chair.

I scooted closer to the table. "Old man, you look good."

He cleared his throat and sucked his teeth.

I giggled and pinched his chin as he gripped my palm to kiss my hand.

Our waitress set a menu in front of me. "Welcome to Melba's. I'm Melissa, your waitress for tonight."

"Hi, Melissa. Can I get a glass of water please?"

"You usually have a glass of wine or something," Dad mentioned.

Melissa made a note. "Sure, a glass of water. Are you two ready to order now?"

"Uhm, I will get a salad and lasagna." I passed the menu back to her.

"Anything for you, sir?" Melissa finished writing my order.

"I'll go for the mac and cheese, greens, cornbread, and baked chicken," Dad ordered, then lifted his menu toward her.

Melissa took both menus and went to another table.

"What?"

Dad tapped my hand playfully. "How are things? We haven't talked in a few days."

"Things are good. I'm busy at work." If I told him about Joey and Darlene, Dad would go up to the job and fight them. That would cause more problems I didn't need.

He folded his hands like a boxer and pretended to throw his fists. "Any knuckleheaded boys I need to beat up?"

"No, Daddy. Stop trying to fight everybody." Like always, he's been my protector and I appreciated him for always being there.

"Your pops got hands, baby."

I glanced around the restaurant at all of the food, still a little nauseous. "What about you in the dating field?"

"Dating is subjective."

I chortled and thanked Melissa as she placed my water down on the table. "Who's driving you crazy now? Let me guess. Myrtle, Sandra, or Cassandra from church?" I rambled, reaching for the water.

He sighed and sipped on his drink. "They want commitment, and Dad isn't marrying again."

I reached to cup his hand, and he caressed my palm. "Dad, you've been single for over twenty years. Mom would want you happy."

"I know, but I'm not ready for that. I like it just you and me."

"Well, what if I told you I wanted to meet someone and get married one day and have a family?" The grin on my face fell at his frown.

"Is there someone I need to know about?"

"No, wel-l," I stuttered and fidgeted in my seat.

He turned his face, cupped his ear, and leaned forward. "Speak up, little girl."

"Nothing to tell."

"Umm... huh."

"Anyway, is Collierville treating you well?" I changed the subject to avoid more talks of having babies.

"You should think of moving down there. Accounting clients are everywhere."

"We'd get on each other's nerves, Daddy."

He smiled, covering my hand with his palm. "Says who?"

Melissa came back over with our food, and he ordered another drink. I stuck my fork in my lasagna and gulped down the first taste. After three hours of conversation and having dessert, we finished and talked about me visiting him soon in Collierville. Once again, he brought up me moving, but I had no plans.

Chapter 5

Maddux

I parked my bike and removed my helmet to meet my brother and the boys at the bar. As soon as I pushed open the door, I heard loud laughter pointing me in the direction of our group. Mykelti extended his hand for a shake, followed by Cairo, Soaquan, and Bishop. The place was simple with a pool table, music, and TVs on the walls. The owners are former navy like us, and they opened the place to give us somewhere to hang out after a mission.

"Where's Aydin?"

Cairo tilted his head toward the bar. "Bar."

I glanced at the bartender giving him cash back as I pulled out a chair to sit down.

"What's up, little brother?" Mykelti asked.

I grabbed a few peanuts from the bowl. "Busting criminals when I can. What about you?"

"Mom told me you were in Pleasantville."

"It wasn't just a mission he got caught up with," Soaquan brought up.

I flipped him off.

Mykelti sipped on his beer. "What are you talking about?" He waved the empty bottle in the air toward the server.

I snatched a beer from Aydin. "Soaquan's just talking."

Soaquan wiggled his brows and flicked the lighter for his cigar.

"Did you meet someone?" Mykelti asked.

The thought made my throat ache with regret from not getting her last name. Was it wise to sleep with her and leave with no trace of saying goodbye?

"I'm not staying too long. Amelia is waiting on me." Aydin stood on the side of the table between Cairo and Soaquan.

"We never get together just the boys," Bishop complained.

"Awww, is Bishop missing his best friends?" I joked.

"Fuck off." Bishop gulped his drink as we burst into laughter.

Soaquan clapped me on the back with a wide grin. "Mykelti, don't let Maddux fool you. He met this sexy girl in Pleasantville."

"You get her number?" Mykelti inquired, then gulped down his drink.

"My love life is not up for discussion."

"Boring," Soaquan groaned and went to the bar.

"So, Columbo put out a few feelers in Interpol," I said to change the subject.

"Victor wants us to keep this under wraps as much as possible," Aydin replied.

I rose from my seat and turned to him. "If we can't handle this job on our own..."

"Then we'll bring in backup," Aydin responded,

reaching into his pocket and tossing a few dollars on the table. He clapped me on the back and walked out.

"How dangerous is this guy?" Mykelti probed.

"He's one of the worst who doesn't care about your family."

Mykelti flipped open his wallet and removed a fifty to pay. "Be careful, bro."

I slapped hands with him again, then we changed the subject and watched Soaquan make a fool of himself as he tried to pick up another woman. After two hours of hanging out, we departed. I went home alone, showered, and fell in bed, thinking of Chanel again.

* * *

The next morning, I groaned as my phone and alarm went off. I rolled over, pushed the covers back, and saw it was eight in the morning. Turning both off, I stared at the end of the bed to get my head together.

Knock! Knock!

I brushed a hand down my face. "Ughhh!" I jumped out of bed, slipped on a shirt, robe, and shoes then marched to the door.

Soaquan held a cup in front of me. "Coffee."

Soaquan, Aydin, and Cairo stood at the door.

I snatched the coffee from him. "Do you know what time it is?" I held the door open. "Shit this is good."

Cairo moved around me and walked inside. "Rayo hit another boat."

"That must be the look of someone that didn't get laid last night." Soaquan smiled.

I shut the door behind me and shook my head to fully wake up. "Let me jump in the shower."

Soaquan waved his hand in front of his face like my breath smelled. "Please, for our sakes."

I blew out a hot breath in his face and chuckled, setting my coffee on the table. Soaquan played the tough role, but we've had a few arguments in the past that Cairo had to break up.

"Go on bro, brush your funky breath." He pushed me back, then propped his feet up on my table.

I went to the bathroom, brushed my teeth, then hopped in the shower. Ten minutes later, I changed into jeans and a black shirt, then heard my stomach grumble.

"Where did he hit?" I questioned as I stepped back in the living room and grabbed my drink.

Soaquan sat up, staring at his phone. "They might be hitting another location," he said.

I trekked to the kitchen and picked up the loaf of bread and popped a slice in the toaster. "Who did they rob?"

"Some prime minister's son!" Cairo yelled.

"Shit." The toast popped up. I grabbed jam and a knife, then plastered jam on top and took a bite before heading back to the living room.

Aydin handed Soaquan's cell back to him. "It's escalating fast."

"He doesn't care," I muttered and sat across on the other couch. The world was a jungle and only the strong would survive unless we could get more people on board with the belief that new criminals had taken things to a higher level.

"Two people died," Cairo said.

Soaquan rose from the chair, glancing out the window. "International crimes."

"Wait to see what the president is going to say," Aydin responded.

I wiped my hand on the napkin and picked up my keys. "Are they taking the case from us?"

"Not yet, so we need to be prepared. Victor is keeping us updated," Aydin mentioned.

"I want this guy now." I slammed my hand on the table.

Cairo ambled to the front door. "He won't get away with this for too long," he remarked.

I got up from the chair. "We need to get to the office for a meeting." I finished my coffee and tossed it in the trash by the door. I locked up and jumped in the truck with Cairo, who drove us to work.

* * *

"Mr. President, we can't rely on these few men to solve this problem," Assistant National Security Advisor Ferman Jones said.

"With all due respect, Mr. Jones, our team is the best to find him." Aydin stood in front of the conference table and stared at the screen with the president, advisor, and secretary of defense on call.

"Where are we with locating him?" Ferman challenged.

"We think he's working with a few contacts from Moses's people," I said, and all eyes turned toward me.

"Who are you?" Ferman asked.

I sat up straight. I wanted to put this man in the middle of what we deal with on a daily basis, but men like him in suits couldn't handle one day on the job. "I'm leading this case."

He narrowed his eyes and whispered in the president's ear. "How are you prepared to handle this if Rayo is still killing people?" Ferman pressed.

"Columbo is working on a few tips from Interpol."

"That's not enough. We have an international problem that looks bad on the president and this country," Ferman growled.

I pointed between me, Cairo, and Aydin. "With all due respect, you're not us."

"Maddux." Aydin shook his head at me, ever the diplomat.

I raised my hand. "Aydin, he has no clue what we do and how we protect this country every day, putting our lives on the line." I jumped up and pointed at the flag in the corner of the room.

"Madduc—" Ferman tried to interrupt me and throw his weight around.

I mumbled under my breath, and balled up my fist as Aydin cleared his throat and pat me on the shoulder. "No, either you provide what we need to handle this case or get out of our way."

"Rayo will make a mistake, they all do," Aydin said.

President Thomas looked at Ferman, then the secretary, then back to Aydin. "I'm giving you another chance with whatever you need. Don't make me regret this, Aydin."

Aydin nudged me to sit down. "You won't, Mr. President."

"Young man." President Thomas stared at me. The entire room faced the screen with their attention focused on the president. Some of the public backlash with the administration ran high and low, but as a SEAL team we had taken an oath.

"Yes, sir." I stood with my head held high.

President Thomas smiled. "I commend you for not backing down."

I glanced at Aydin and Cairo. "I learned from the best."

Finally our call ended, and I sat back down and released the breath I held as the president spoke to me. Serving your country and having the pleasure of the Commander-in-Chief being aware of your team was the best feeling in the world.

"All right, Maddux, you're up," Aydin informed.

I rubbed my chin and sighed. "I hate Ferman."

Soaquan chuckled, placing the cup of water down before flipping through the pictures. "He wants to run for president."

"I wouldn't put it past him," I answered.

"He has a point though," Cairo said.

My jaw went slack with worry. "What point exactly?"

"If we can't catch Rayo, we need to step aside and let Homeland bring in someone else." Cairo's lip curled into a frown.

"Rayo's not a ghost. He's going to make mistakes. I've studied him the longest." Aydin walked to the table and hit something on the computer, bringing up a map. He treaded over to the screen and pointed at a picture of Rayo. "Our number one suspect is Rayo."

"Family?" I asked.

"Everyone's littered around the world," Soaquan replied.

"They stole over a million dollars from the prime minister's son," Cairo read from the file.

I snapped my fingers and gestured to more evidence of Rayo's destruction in Italy. "The Italian prime minister wants blood." Although we remained calm at all missions, when kids and women were used and abused it did something to us. The bodies of people in Italy discovered at the hands of Rayo cut deep. The picture changed to the prime minister and his family.

"We can get the president to tap into the CIA database," Aydin explained.

"Rayo is making a lot of enemies."

"He doesn't know what's coming," Cairo warned.

Confrontation with murderers comes with the job and I hoped and prayed it sent a message to other evils in the world that we stood up to bullies, and nameless and faceless cruelty can never prevail.

Chapter 6

Chanel

Four weeks later

The past week had been stressful. I worked extra hours to make up for Joey assigning some of my clients to Darlene, which made things even more difficult at the office. On top of that I'd been feeling under the weather. I promised to meet a client for lunch to discuss her needs for her business. I walked behind the hostess toward the table at Pink's restaurant and bar. They served the best food in the city.

"Do you want to order drinks now?" the hostess asked.

I removed my coat and laid it on the back of the chair. "Uhm, I can wait a few minutes."

"All right, your waitress will be out shortly."

"Thanks." I scanned the area. It wasn't too crowded for midday, and I was thankful I could have a few moments to get myself together. I grabbed my compact out of my purse and checked my makeup and hair.

"Focus, Chanel."

The second I finished this meeting, I was going straight home to sleep off the day.

"Chanel! Thank you for meeting me." Donna was a picture of elegance in a black pantsuit. Her thick hair spilled around the delicate bones of her face and slim figure. She probably stayed in the gym.

I glanced up and smiled at Donna. I started to rise out of my seat, but she waved me off.

Donna put her bag on the back of her chair. She wore a perfume that held notes of musk and sweet. It was strong and I felt it in my throat. As bad as I wanted to cancel I knew I couldn't.

I glanced to the ceiling briefly to control my emotions so I could focus. "How are you doing?"

Donna grinned, giving me a once-over. "Good. Excited to be meeting finally."

"Hi, I'm Lenard. I'll be your waiter today. Get you started with drinks?"

"Can I get a glass of water?"

"Water and you, ma'am?" he asked Donna.

"I'll have water as well. Are you ready to order, Chanel?"

"I can go for the ravioli and salad."

"That sounds good. I'll get the same, with parmesan cheese," Donna answered, and Lenard wrote on his notepad.

"Two raviolis and two salads. Water will be right up," he confirmed and walked off.

"So, tell me what your thoughts are." Donna clasped her hands together.

"I think expanding is good. You're in a unique position to grow."

Donna bobbed her head in excitement. "I'm glad you agree. I want to open more stores."

"It can be done. My only concern is taking on too much equity too fast."

"The locations I checked out looked reasonable." Donna typed on her phone and showed me her notes.

I gripped my stomach and felt queasy again. Lenard approached and placed two glasses of water on the table. I grabbed mine and took a large gulp.

"Are you all right? You look kind of pale," Donna questioned.

I shook my head. "I think I'm coming down with something."

Donna craned her neck and frowned. "Oh, sorry to hear that. You do look a little tired."

"Work stress."

She reached in her purse and removed a bottle of lotion. "I've been there."

"Food is coming right out," Lenard said, then moved to another table.

"Yeah. I need you to make sure the records are sent to me."

Again my stomach had a mind of its own and grumbled like I needed to throw up. "Not a problem."

Lenard returned and placed our food on the table, and the smell of the parmesan cheese turned my stomach.

I turned my head and closed my eyes for a second, my throat ready to erupt. "Excuse me, I need to go to the restroom." I got out of the chair.

"No worries."

I marched to the bathroom, pushed the stall open, and everything I had for breakfast came out.

What is happening to me?

I lay against the stall door and felt my forehead for a

fever. Standing, I stumbled to the sink, turned on the faucet, and washed my hands.

"Take advice from me. Next time, just tell him no." The woman next to me laughed.

"Excuse me?"

"You just threw up. You seem flustered and ready to pass out. I've been there three times."

"Three times?"

She giggled, tossing the napkins in the trash. "Oh honey, you don't know?"

I shook my head.

"Pregnant."

I blinked repeatedly, not comprehending what she said. "Preg...nant?"

"Look at the upside, at least you had fun making the baby."

She chuckled, turned, and left the bathroom. I stared at the mirror, closed my eyes, and recalled the last time I had a period. "Right before the *boat trip*."

The door flew open, and two more women stepped inside, laughing together.

"I can't be pregnant." My mind had blocked out the short conversation with Moria, because it was never a thought, but I had also ignored the changes in certain foods I usually loved.

Slowly, I sauntered back to the table.

Donna continued to text on her phone. "Hey, you don't look so good."

"Uhm. I need to cut the meeting short."

"What's wrong?"

I picked up my purse, briefcase, and cell. "Nothing major. I'm just feeling under the weather." I slid out my wallet.

Donna stood and extended her arms for a hug. "The bill is on me. Feel better, and we'll talk when you're ready."

"Thanks, Donna. Send over the budget, and I'll get started on it as soon as possible."

I rushed out of the restaurant and to my car, frantically rethinking my timeline of over the last few months. The only one I could come up with was Maddux on the boat.

The light turned green, and I sped down the street overthinking what I've done to myself. When I got home, I dumped everything on the bed with the tests I had and picked up each box to read the instructions. A few seconds after peeing on each stick, I washed my hands and watched the timer that would decide if my life would change in the blink of an eye.

Ding!

Slowly, I leaned over the counter and looked at the two tests. Both showed lines that indicated a positive pregnancy.

I stumbled back, hand on my stomach. "Pregnant."

Buzz!

"I'm pregnant." The thought of a baby, being someone's mother.

Buzz!

I marched out of the bathroom, grabbed the phone from my bed, and saw Rose's name across the screen.

"Hey." I cleared my throat.

"Hey... What's the matter?"

Suddenly I felt overwhelmed and breathless. "I'm not sure."

"Are you hurt?"

I lay back on the bed and blew out a frustrated breath. "Worse." I lifted my legs to my chest, turning into a fetal position. My dad was going to kill me.

"Chanel, what's the problem?"

"Rose, I'm pregnant."

She laughed.

"I'm not joking."

Rose cleared her throat. "How can you be pregnant, Chanel?"

"When a guy and a girl get together and have sex…"

"I know about sex. Who's the father?" she snapped.

"Maddux."

A sharp gasp escaped her. "The sexy guy from the boat?"

"Yeah."

"Wow." Was she mad? I mean we talked about her wanting a family before me and had mapped out her future.

I laid flat on my back and put the phone on speaker. "What am I going to do?"

"Wow." Rose got quiet.

"Rose!" I yelled.

"Huh?"

Aggravated at her quietness I sat up and leaned against the headboard. "I work long hours, sometimes sixty hours a week. Plus, my father is going to kill me."

Rose smacked her lips. "Chanel, you're not sixteen. You're thirty."

I slid from the bed. "That's not the point. I envisioned being married with a dog and a front yard."

"Life has a way of showing you that you can't plan everything out. What are you going to do?"

I ambled to the bathroom and cleaned up. "I have no way of getting in touch with Maddux."

"He's Bria's friend. Maybe try to call her."

Maddux had probably forgotten about me.

"He's most likely across the world by now. Bria has

enough going on without me putting my problems off on her and Cairo."

"He deserves to know, Chanel."

I flicked the light off after washing my hands. "I know, but I need to confirm everything and have time to process my emotions."

"Well, I'm going to start a baby registry and get some names started," Rose joked.

"Ugh, I thought you'd be a little more serious."

Rose cheered. "You're having a baby. That's the best news of all time. Me being a sexy auntie."

"How did I not know you'd make this about you."

"Never underestimate me."

Beep!

I pulled the phone from my ear. "I'm getting another call. I'll talk later."

"Okay, love you loads."

"You too." I smiled at the sight of my father's name and clicked over. "Hi, Daddy."

"Glad you remembered your old father."

I chortled, as I changed into slippers. "I could never forget the best man in my life."

"What are you up to?"

I sauntered out of my bedroom and headed to the kitchen, opening the fridge for a bottle of water. "Home from a business meeting and talking with Rose."

"You two owe me dinner this week."

I sat against the counter, staring out the window. "I promise I'll make sure to be there this time."

"Job treating you right?" he probed.

"No, but I want to hear about you."

"Whose ass do I need to kick?" he growled.

I dropped down on the couch and lifted the TV remote.

"No one, just an account I lost." I sighed, dragging a hand down my face. My mood was becoming worse by the minute without confirmation from a doctor if I was pregnant. Keeping the secret from my father was just as hard.

"I won't hold you up. Call me tomorrow when you're on your way to me," Dad said.

"I promise," I replied, then ended the call. I scrolled through my phone and started to call my doctor to make an appointment when I heard loud music playing.

I jumped up and stomped to the front door. "What in the world?" Yanking it open, I saw boxes lined up on the side of the wall.

"A new neighbor," I mumbled and marched two doors down and raised my hand to knock when the door opened, and a beautiful woman smiled.

"Hi," she said.

"Hello. I'm a few doors from you. Are you new in the building?"

She nodded, extending her hand. "I am. Vanessa."

I grabbed her palm. "Chanel. Do you mind turning the music down a little?"

Vanessa grinned and cupped the doorknob. "Sorry. I got caught up in moving and needed a distraction."

"No problem, just had a long day at work."

Vanessa walked away and turned down the volume.

I stood at the entrance and glanced around her living room. "Your place is beautiful."

"Thanks. I'm still getting everything settled."

"Love the color scheme."

Her layout was a replica of mine with a kitchen and living room, high ceilings, and a fireplace.

She gestured around at the furniture. "Decorating is my passion."

"It shows."

Vanessa pat her forehead, then snapped her fingers. "Hey, I'm actually going to a party tonight. Do you want to join me?"

"I doubt I'd be the best person to bring to a party."

"Come on, my job is boring sometimes, and you'd be doing me a favor."

"If you say so."

Vanessa walked to the TV and turned it off. "Great, put on something cute."

"Where's the party?"

She grinned and jumped up and down in excitement. "On a massive yacht. As a model, it comes with some perks."

I felt the tightness in my throat at her answer. "A yacht."

Chapter 7

Chanel

I resisted the urge to turn around and go back home to sleep off my problems. Vanessa wore a one-piece suit with a skirt and no top. I put on leggings, crop top, and flat sandals. I wasn't planning to drink and just wanted to hang around and distract myself from what was going on. I expected the boat to be the same size as the one I was on with Bria and Cairo, but this one was way larger.

"Who owns this boat?" I asked, accepting a bottle of water from the waiter.

"One of the perks of being a model in high fashion." Vanessa grinned, picking a glass of champagne from the other waiter's tray.

"It's a mega yacht, worth at least forty million dollars." Vanessa described as she motioned to the front deck. "They have a pool on the back deck."

"We can sit on the inside."

"What do they have on board?"

Vanessa escorted me down the hall to the interior of the yacht. "They say it has a library, theater, and spa."

"I could live here," I joked, as we sat on the plush seats.

Loud music blasted around us, and guys and girls danced together and talked.

"How long have you been a model?" I inquired, sipping on the water.

Vanessa waved at a group of guys standing near the bar. "About four years now. I moved from France."

I reared back. "France! How was that?"

She laughed it off. "It's France. Beautiful city and people and delicious food. I got a contract here and needed to move."

"Family?"

"I grew up in Ohio and moved to France when I got started. My family supports me."

"That's impressive."

"Thanks, but tell me more about you. When you came to my door, I felt like your energy was off."

I nodded in acknowledgement. "I've just gotten some news, and my mind has been on an emotional roller-coaster."

The door flew open, and a group of men with guns smiled then licked their lips.

"Ahhh!" a few women screamed.

"What do we have here?" A man with long, curly hair, chestnut skin tone, and tattoos on his bare arms and neck approached a woman and caressed her cheek.

"Please, don't kill me," she pleaded.

He laughed and gripped her by the chin, yanking her by the neck to his chest. "Adolph, I told you we'd get more than just money this time," he announced as I glanced between the two men.

"Sir, take whatever you want. We don't want any trouble," a guy in shorts and no shirt spoke up.

A gun cocked. *Pop!*

"Arghhhh!" I screamed and jumped back, shocked at someone being killed in front of me.

"Pussy," the leader taunted, shoving the women to the floor.

His eyes scanned the room, then he stepped to the bar, grabbed a bottle of liquor, and drank. "We're the Cavente Gang. We come in peace," he joked, and his men laughed.

Whimpers and cries were heard.

"I'm Rayo, and I'm your new captain."

Something about him made me believe I wasn't getting off this boat alive. I remembered my phone in my purse, and I slid my hand inside, watching as his men focused and kept the guns pointed around the room.

"I give the orders. Today, we want all of your money and what's in the safe."

"There's no money on board!" an older man with gray hair shouted.

Rayo pointed the gun in his direction. "Who are you?"

"I'm the person in charge." He held a tormented stare, recognizing what was at stake.

"Wrong answer." Rayo punched him in the face.

"Fuck!" he cursed and covered his nose with his hand as blood seeped out.

Rayo walked by each person, stopping at a man in a long white shirt and shorts. "Who are you?"

He kept his eyes low, hands up in the air. "Umm, Kent, and we don't have money or a safe."

Rayo licked his lips. "Well, Kent, I guess you'll die."

"Wait! Wait!" Kent begged for his life.

"Speak," Rayo growled, shoving the gun under Kent's chin.

"This is only a rented yacht. We don't own it."

"So, you're pretending to be wealthy to uhhh... impress ladies."

Kent shook his head. "No, it's a company party. I work for Atlantic Fashion Magazine." Kent tried to reach in his pocket.

Rayo nudged the gun farther under his throat.

"I don't have a weapon. It's my business card."

Rayo reached into Kent's pocket and gripped the wallet, tossing cards on the floor. "Kent Walton, Creative Director," Rayo remarked, whistling.

"I promise if you let us go, we can forget this happened."

Ring!

All heads turned toward me, and I tensed and raised my hands in the air. Rayo's men stomped toward me, snatching me up by my arm.

"I wasn't doing anything!" I shouted and stumbled over my heel.

Vanessa tried to reach out for me. Rayo slapped her across the face.

"Oh my God!" I shouted.

One of his men shoved me and stole the phone. "She was trying to call for help."

"No, that's not true," I begged.

Rayo looked me up and down. "Are you trying to leave when we're having so much fun?" he questioned.

I shook my head, looking back at Vanessa.

"Take them both down to the rooms."

"Wait, no, please," I pleaded.

His men started to drag me away by my arm, but Rayo snapped his fingers, and they stopped. "You have something to say?"

"Look, take the money and jewelry. But I'm pregnant. Please don't hurt us."

He smirked, rubbed his chin, and grazed a finger down my cheek. "I like them pregnant."

"You're disgusting!" Vanessa shouted. Rayo cocked his gun and pointed it at her.

Boom!

Smoke appeared out of nowhere.

Pop! Pop!

Everyone on the boat dropped to the floor as the windows broke, and guns went off. I crawled to get my purse, moving behind the bar to try to dial out, but there was no signal.

"This is the United States Coast Guard, along with the US Navy. Put your guns down."

"Fuck you!" Rayo sent fire back and ran with some of his men toward the windows. They leaned up to look around and saw the rescue team.

"Vanessa!" I ran toward her as she slowly tried to stand. She had been shot in the side.

"Mmmm... it hurts," she cried.

"Help! She needs help!" I yelled, and a few guys rushed in with medical bags. I stepped back to allow them to work on her. I rubbed my arms with my hands, praying she'd be okay.

"Chanel?"

I heard that voice and thought I was in another universe. "Maddux?"

He rushed toward me and pulled me to his chest. "Are you hurt?" He scrubbed his hands up and down my body to check for wounds.

I pointed at Vanessa. "I'm fine. Vanessa needs help the most."

Maddux glared at me, then straightened a little as he walked around the room. "What are you doing here?"

"I..."

"Maddux! They took off."

He approached us with a piece of paper in his hand.

"He can't get far," Maddux replied.

"Is she all right?" his friend asked.

Maddux laid a hand on my lower back. "This is Chanel, the woman I told you about."

"I'm Aydin. Nice to meet you, Chanel." Aydin extended a hand.

I shook it. "Nice to meet you."

"I need to finish checking things out. I'll take you home." Maddux looked completely different in all of his work gear. He was already sexy in jeans and a shirt, but his sexiness only intensified that I wanted to fuck him right now.

Getting invited to a party to end up almost being kidnapped and killed after finding out I was pregnant put things into perspective. I wanted my baby and couldn't imagine life without them after this experience.

I bent down to grab my purse. "I can get home fine. You don't have to worry about me." I needed space before I threw up again and he learned my secret.

Maddux cupped my arm, tilted my chin up, and stared into my eyes.

"I will take you home. Give me a minute to talk with my team."

"Okay."

He winked and brushed the back of his hand against my chin. I sat on the couch as they wrapped up Vanessa and prepared to remove her from the boat. She extended her palm, and I gripped her hand.

"I'm right behind you."

I looked up at Aydin and Maddux as they talked with other men who were holding guns and dressed in bullet-proof vests and headsets. I walked behind the EMTs carrying out Vanessa. Maddux glanced at me.

"Chanel."

"I was going to make sure Vanessa was okay."

"They're the best in the field. We're leaving now. I can take you home."

I looked behind him as his people directed guests to leave. "You don't need to stay with your team?"

Maddux shifted and escorted me toward the boat next to the yacht. "No, our work is finished for now." He helped me climb on. They started the engine and pulled off.

* * *

Maddux walked me to my door, and I slid the key inside, kicked off my shoes, and dropped my purse on the couch. I sat and raised my hands to my face, overwhelmed with what was going on after we left Vanessa at the hospital. Tears pooled in my eyes.

"Hey, shush... don't worry. She's going to be fine." Maddux sat next to me and wrapped me in his arms.

I wiped my eyes and stared into his, then down to his lips, and the urge to kiss him popped into my head.

He rubbed my cheek.

I leaned in and pressed a kiss to his lips. "I'm sorry." I jumped up and paced in front of him.

Maddux pat the seat next to him. "You seem way more upset than I am. Hey, come sit down."

I blew out a breath and shook my hands. "I'm preg-nant," I blurted, fidgeting with my fingers.

His brow dipped in confusion. "Congrats."

My head jerked back. "Huh?" I knew we just came from a traumatizing event, but his flippant non emotional congrats irritated me.

He scratched the back of his head. "Congrats to your new baby."

"You're the father," I mumbled, propped my hands on my sides, and watched as his body tensed.

"Father of what?"

"I'm pregnant with your child."

"How? W-we..." he stuttered and jumped up, pacing in front of me.

I placed a hand on his shoulder. "Listen, I know this is tough. I can't believe it either."

"How far along?"

"Well, I don't know exactly."

Maddux jerked his head toward me. "What do you mean? You went to a doctor, right?"

"Not yet. I just found out earlier today."

"You took a test?"

I sat on the loveseat. "Two." His constant questions felt like daggers to the heart.

"Shit."

"Listen, if it's confirmed, I'm not looking for a handout or anything."

Maddux paused, his mouth opening and closing before he got himself together. "Chanel, don't insult me like that."

"Some guys freak out when it's a one-night stand."

He dropped to his knee. "Never compare me to those guys."

I released the breath I was holding.

Maddux picked up my hand and squeezed. "Sorry, it's a lot to take in and then the boat situation." He removed his phone and typed before looking back at me. "Rayo Cavente." Maddux stood and put his hands in his pocket.

"Who?"

"They're on the FBI and Interpol watch list as gun smugglers and pirates."

"*Pirates?*" I asked, crossing my arms.

"Basically, big-time robbers, who kill if they need to."

I bit my fingernail, anxiety rising high as the events of today replayed. Maddux filled me in on what his days had been like for the weeks after we left each other. We talked more if I was hurt at all and making an appointment with the doctor.

Chapter 8

Maddux

We sat outside a brick one-story house that was used as one of Rayo's many gun trafficking locations. The file I received showed most of Rayo's crew came in and out throughout the day. They didn't have one spot as the set base, they traveled around the world, but we noticed through Columbo's investigation that every few months, one of Rayo's men would come here to meet a woman. We found out his girlfriend worked as a bank teller. Lourdes Sanchez didn't seem like the type to be with someone who had a hand in crime, but you could never be surprised. I lifted the binoculars and watched as she parked and grabbed a few grocery bags from the car then locked the door. I checked my watch and saw it was going on five in the afternoon. He normally showed up at this time with money and gifts.

"How are you feeling?"

"About?" I lowered the binoculars and looked over at Aydin in the passenger seat. Cairo and Bishop were seated in the back.

"What that girl said about you being a father?" Bishop asked.

I couldn't avoid that conversation with my team any longer, even though this was the worst time to spill my feelings. I mean I didn't even know how I felt about everything and still hadn't called Chanel back. I was in New York for a few days doing surveillance on the Cavente crew with Senate Leaders, then we had to fly back to Nashville.

"I honestly can't say how I feel right now other than shocked."

Bishop raised his camera to snap photos. "When we rescued her on the boat, she seemed familiar."

"That was the girl I met at Bria and Cairo's party."

"Bria asked me if you talked to Chanel," Cairo said.

I nodded but before I could answer, a car roared down the street. It pulled into Lourdes' driveway.

"Let's give him a little wiggle room." I stared as Miquel stepped out of the Durango.

"Columbo get any information on how many people live here?" I asked as I flipped through the files in the folder on my lap.

"A total of three people," Cairo explained.

"Lourdes, her brother, and uncle," I read from the report on the property.

Bishop reloaded his camera. "After this, we should get some food," he muttered.

My stomach grumbled in agreement. We'd been on the stakeout for the past three hours after hitting up every spot we thought Rayo's men would hang out.

"Miquel is one of the men Rayo trusts, so we have to be careful."

I glanced at Aydin. "You think it's a setup?"

I tapped on the steering wheel and peered at the front

door. "I want him alive so we can get some information."
Aydin removed his seatbelt.

I checked the gun on my left hip and went to open the door. "Unless he gives us reason not to keep him alive."

We all climbed out of the car. It was mid-to-late afternoon, in a mostly family area with kids playing outside. The team couldn't cause too much destruction and have neighbors call the police. Cavente's crew would go deeper into hiding. I rang the doorbell and heard a dog barking, a loud TV, and someone yelling.

The locks turned, and the door opened to Miquel. He tried to shut it, and I stuck my foot in before he could get it closed.

"What the fuck!" he shouted.

I pushed the door open, and he fell into the wall. I pulled out my gun, pointed it at him and who I assumed was Lourdes' uncle Leo. "Don't be stupid, Miquel."

"What do you want?" he asked, his hands up.

"Where's Rayo?" I gritted my teeth and gripped his neck with the gun under his chin.

Miquel shook his head.

"Arghhh! Let him go!" Lourdes screamed and tried to run up on me.

Cairo stepped in front of me.

"Tell us what we need to know, Miquel, or you'll be spending the rest of your life in jail."

Miquel's chest heaved up and down and his mouth pressed in a thin line. "I haven't talked to Rayo."

"So, you had nothing to do with the robbery on the boat a week ago?"

His eyes scanned from Lourdes to Uncle Leo sitting in the chair. The living room was clean—like a normal family lived here. From the photos Columbo was able to send us, they had people in and out of the house at all hours of the night, parties on the weekends, and even some kids at one point.

I moved the gun from him to Lourdes. "If you think Lourdes is going to stick around for a lifetime, think about it."

"Miquel is innocent!" Lourdes shouted, trying to push Cairo back to approach us.

I chuckled. "You have her fooled."

Miquel gritted his teeth. "I don't know what you're talking about."

I squeezed his jaw, released my grip, and stepped back. "Rayo is going down. It's a matter of who takes the fall with him."

Aydin peered over at me, and I chucked up my head. We all turned to leave the house and treaded back to the car. Miquel stood at the front door and watched as the Tahoe drove away. I pulled my phone out of my pocket and sent a message that I'd been nervous to send.

Me: *Dinner tonight?*
Chanel: *I'd like that.*

I relaxed back in the seat as Bishop grumbled about the next step in capturing Rayo. "He's toying with us."

"Rayo can't make any mistakes right now. More than likely, he'll make contact with Miquel," I said.

* * *

My mind raced and heart beat fast because this wasn't something I wanted to deal with, not that I regretted sleeping with Chanel, but becoming a father from this situation would have my parents disappointed in me.

"Hi."

I looked up from my phone and peered at Chanel. A lump formed in my throat. She was mesmerizing, and just as beautiful as the first day we met. I prayed if we had a girl she looked just like her mother, which meant she couldn't date until she was forty.

I stood up, chuckled, and pulled out her chair. "Sorry, I have a habit of staring."

She smiled and sat, placing her keys and clutch on the table. "Nice place."

"Thanks, I figured you'd know the place since you're from the surrounding area."

"Never been here before," Chanel replied as she laid her napkin on her lap. Our waitress came to our table with two wine glasses. The way Chanel was dressed right now, I wish we'd talked sooner. She was glowing and it only made me want to take her on top of this table. Her lips were covered in a bright red, and the scent of light vanilla flowed to my nose, warm and inviting.

"I already ordered wine, but we can just have water."

"It's fine. You go ahead and drink."

The waitress hesitated before pouring.

"Are you sure? I don't want you to feel left out."

"Yes, the doctor said a little won't hurt, but I'll have water. I have an appointment with my doctor soon."

"You've already booked to meet the doctor?"

"Do you need me to come back?" the waitress asked.

"Yes—"

"No—"

"I'll give you two a minute."

"What did the doctor say?"

Chanel smiled, reached in her purse, and pulled out a piece of paper. "That I'm pregnant, around two months."

Shocked, I sat back in my chair, mouth dropping open. I stared over the sonogram.

Chanel cupped my hand with a comforting expression. "This wasn't something planned."

"Right, it is life-changing..."

"I know guys think we try to trap them. But this wasn't what I envisioned for my life either," Chanel rambled on.

I held up my hand to stop her from talking nonsense. My parents didn't raise deadbeat fathers. Am I surprised? Shocked? A hundred percent, but I would never leave a child in the world that had my blood running through its veins.

"Tell me what the doctor said."

"Basically, I was coming along nicely and I should continue keeping my stress down."

"What stress?"

The mention of stress and someone harming her or my child caused a tightness in my chest.

Chanel watched from the front entrance back to me. "After the boat situation, I've been on edge a little."

I reached across the table and covered her hand with mine. "Hey, I promise I will get them. Rayo won't hurt you."

"How is that going?" She smiled.

The waitress stepped back to our table and pulled out the pen. "Have we decided on what to order?"

"Yeah, can I get steak and fettuccine." I handed the menu to her.

"Do you have ravioli and tomato soup?" Chanel inquired.

"We do, would you like that?"

"Is that one of those baby cravings?" I joked.

Chanel closed the menu and passed it to the waitress. "Shut up, this baby has my appetite in a knot."

Our waitress walked away to put in the orders. More guests entered the restaurant, and light conversation filled in the air.

"What did your parents think?"

She cleared her throat and patted her chest. "I haven't told my dad yet."

"Why not?"

Chanel's voice cracked. "After my mom died, it's been just the two of us. And I'm afraid to disappoint him."

"He can't be mad, it's not like you're sixteen and pregnant. You're a grown woman." No one, not even my parents, would disrespect her or my child, so I'd be damned if her father tried to come at her the wrong way.

She sighed, nodded, then smiled as the waitress brought our meals over.

"Steak and fettuccine. Ravioli and soup for you," she muttered and filled my wine glass.

"Thank you," we both answered.

I picked up the steak knife and cut into my food.

Chanel lifted her fork. "No, but I didn't plan on being unwed and pregnant from a casual hookup on a boat."

"That was a crazy day."

She blushed, closing her eyes. "Yes, it was."

I smirked and tapped her hand. "I don't regret what happened on the boat."

"You sure?"

She deserved to be treated like a queen, baby in the picture or not. She made me feel comfortable and open on the boat.

"I still think about you," I confessed.

Chanel cocked her head to the side and palmed her left

cheek. "Please, you're probably dating other women. You don't have to make me feel better."

"Dating is the last thing on my mind. My team is working on the boat robbery case."

"Have you had any leads?"

I didn't want to scare her or get her hopes up. "Normally we don't talk about cases, but you're safe. I promise."

We continued discussing her work and visiting her father soon. I mentioned us both going together moving forward on all appointments and events dealing with the baby.

After dinner I walked her out and waited for the valet to bring her car around. I stood in front of her as she tried to avoid eye contact with me.

"I'm surprised you're not freaking out over the news and dodging me," she admitted, fidgeting with her hands.

I scratched the back of my head. "Honestly, I'm still processing everything, but I'm not stupid enough to deny that we slept together."

Chanel removed a few dollars from her purse to tip. "We can get a DNA test."

I rubbed my chin in thought.

The car pulled up in front of us, and I slipped my hand in my pocket to grab a tip for the valet as he passed her the keys.

"Here you go," I told him.

"You don't have to do that Maddux," she replied.

"If nothing else, I'm a gentleman. My mom would curse me out."

She nodded, put her money back, and stepped around to the driver's side. I followed and held the door open.

She slid inside and pulled on her seatbelt. "I'd feel better if we had a test done."

"Send me the location, and I can have it done and expedited."

"Sure. Thanks again for dinner."

I planted a hand on top of the car and gazed into her eyes. "I want to see you again." I bent down through the open window.

Chanel smirked. "You have my number."

I bit my bottom lip and chuckled. "The team heads back out in a week. Maybe do the DNA test then."

She put the car in drive. "How about after the DNA test, I make us lunch at my place."

"Sounds like a great plan."

I watched as she pulled into traffic. My phone rang, and I slipped it out of my pocket and answered. "Maddux."

"He's on the move here," Bishop said.

"Where are you?"

"Keeping a steady distance on Third and Broadway."

"I'm on my way."

I hung up and held my ticket out for the valet to bring my car around. If Rayo's men were making moves, this could be our big break.

Chapter 9

Chanel

eeks later
We received the results of the DNA test and Maddux is the father. Part of me was ecstatic to have validation even though I knew all along. Rose helped me pick out a few items for the baby's nursery. Maddux would be coming over today for dinner after we had lunch a few days ago. He's to leave for work this weekend so we needed to finalize any last-minute details for the baby.

"I wish you'd find out the baby's gender," Rose fussed, grabbing a few baby bottles from the shelf.

"I'll find out when I go see my dad."

Rose whined and stomped her feet. "That's too long."

I shrugged and stepped around her to pick up the baby wipes. "Maddux wanted to be there, and he left for Memphis."

"Remind Maddux that I'm the godmother so we're on the same page when I spoil them."

I held up a yellow onesie. "He knows, I promise." I

pointed to the wall display of baby toys that showcased colors and animals. "These are cute."

"Have you two discussed where the baby is going to live?"

"Home with me."

She stopped walking, and I bumped into her. "What?"

"Maddux lives in Hendersonville, so he's going to go back and forth?"

Rose frowned, tossing bibs in the basket. "I mean that's the only option right now unless he moves here." She held up two different shampoo brands for the baby. "What about you moving there? Your father is out there."

I dropped the clothes in my basket and continued over to the blanket section in Target. "We have time."

"Chanel the baby will be here before you know it and then you'll have to rearrange your work schedule."

My job was fine with me taking maternity leave, but my clients had increased and it would take a little time to get my coworkers up to date.

"It will all work out."

"Has he said anything about the robbery from the boat? What about your neighbor?"

"Vanessa is recovered. Right now, she's focused on rehab. Maybe we should have a girls' night?" I suggested, checking out the material of blankets.

Finally finished I approached the empty line to pay, pulling out my wallet after handing the clothes to the cashier.

Rose bagged up the products. "Still scary that no one has captured them."

I punched in my code to pay. "The whole situation is crazy, but I trust Maddux will catch up with them."

After we checked out we left the store and loaded everything up in the trunk of the car.

"I'll drive. We should order food."

"A big bowl of ice cream, a burger, steak fries, and pickles." I rubbed my stomach.

Rose pinched her nose like something smelled funny.

"What?" I laughed.

She waved me off. "All these weird cravings from the baby." She reversed out of the parking space and turned out of the area to the main road.

I turned up the radio and listened to her try to sing Mariah Carey. When we arrived, we parked at my place and got out.

The doorman held the door open for us. "Ladies, do you need help?"

I carried three bags. "Thanks, we do if you don't mind."

Rose picked up four while we sauntered to the elevator.

"No problem. Head up, and I'll bring the rest inside." He walked out to the grab the rest.

"Thank you!" I hit the button for the elevator.

As soon as we stepped off the elevator, Vanessa came out of her place with a bag in her hand.

I dropped my bags in front of the door. "How are you feeling?" I asked as I pulled my keys out of my purse.

Vanessa squinted. "Slowly getting better. Taking the trash out and trying to not focus on the pain."

The doors of the elevator opened again, and the doorman brought the rest of my stuff.

"We're about to eat and hang out. Do you want to chill with us?"

Vanessa looked around at all the baby gifts. "You guys don't need me bringing your day down."

I removed the key and pushed the door open, letting

Rose take the bags inside. I took my coat off and hung it on the coatrack. "I don't have any plans until later."

"Are you sure?" Vanessa pressed.

I held up my phone. "Girls' lunch! I'm ordering all the junk food."

"If I'm not intruding, let me drop this off in the trash," Vanessa said.

All the bags were brought in, and I tipped the doorman and closed the door. Rose removed everything, and I ordered our food and closed out of the app. Then my phone rang with Maddux's name.

"Hello." I stood at the back of the couch.

"I got the results." His soothing voice brought me a sense of calm.

I was truly prepared to be a single parent, but somehow he'd taken the reins of being a father and stepped up without me having to demand anything from him.

"How are you feeling?"

Knock!

I moved to let Vanessa in, but Rose jumped up and beat me to the door. I went to my bedroom and kicked off my shoes.

"Exhausted." He yawned.

"We can always reschedule you coming over. I don't want to keep you from getting rest."

"I want to see you."

I slipped off my earrings and placed them in a box. "Okay. Have you told your family?" I waited with bated breath over what he would say.

"No, I will when I get back home."

Was I disappointed? A part of me wanted his family to be as excited as I was. But knowing how things came about with us, I had to respect how their feelings may not be the same. I stepped out of the closet in my house shoes, went back to the living room, and picked up Princess from Rose's arms.

"What time are you coming over?"

"Not too late. I know you have work tomorrow."

"If you have to cancel, I understand."

"Chanel," Maddux grumbled.

"Yeah?" My stomach fluttered.

"I want to see you as much as you want to see me." A smile in his voice perked me up.

I smirked and rolled my eyes at him. "Is this the cocky Maddux coming out again?"

"If nothing else, I'm a gentleman with a little cockiness." He chuckled, and we said goodbye at the same time and hung up.

"Hey, Princess." I rubbed behind Princess' ear.

"How's Maddux?" Rose asked.

Knock! Knock!

"That's the food."

"I got it." Rose sauntered to the door.

"Who's Maddux?" Vanessa sat on the loveseat, picking over the clothes.

I rubbed my stomach. "The father of my little surprise."

"The guy that she slept with on the boat," Rose blurted out and placed the food on the table.

"Rose!" I hissed, putting Princess on the floor.

Vanessa giggled.

Rose pretended to hump the couch. "He literally knocked her up in one night. That's a keeper."

I threw a pillow toward her as we all laughed. "It's the guy who helped us the day of the robbery."

Vanessa grinned. "The one who was about to kill the guy who was trying to touch you?"

I waved off her comment and pulled my food from the container. "He wasn't about to kill anyone."

"Tall, sexy, bowlegged walk, and pretty teeth," Rose bragged about Maddux.

I glared at her. "Focus on your love life." I jumped up and trekked to the kitchen for napkins.

Rose opened a packet of ketchup. "Oops, see? She's already claimed her man. Let me stop."

"Honestly, that's a blessing, Chanel," Vanessa said.

"What is?"

Vanessa popped a fry in her mouth. "Having someone in your corner. My friends, or lack of guy friends, aren't returning any of my calls. My jobs stopped coming in since the incident."

"Sorry to hear that, Vanessa. Don't they know it wasn't your fault? I mean they should give you time to heal."

"I'd expect a miracle at this point to get another gig," Vanessa complained.

"So, they just stopped booking you?" Rose probed.

Vanessa nodded, then bit into her burger. "They told me, and I quote, 'We can't have any liabilities.'"

"That's bullshit. You want something to drink?" Rose asked as she rose from her seat and went to the kitchen.

"Bring me some apple juice," I replied.

"I'll take water," Vanessa answered.

The girls debated on baby names, and we decided to decorate the nursery in the guestroom.

* * *

Three hours later, I stepped out of the shower as my doorbell rang.

"Coming!" I shouted, checked myself in the mirror one more time, and left Princess in my bedroom.

"Hey." My face fell when I saw Maddux had a Band-Aid over his left eye.

Maddux pointed at his cut. "Don't feel bad, I'm fine."

I stepped aside and motioned for him to come in and closed the door behind him. "What happened?" I touched the side of his face, and he winced and stepped out of my hold.

"Fighting the bad guys," he tried to joke as he removed his jacket.

I saw a purple bruise on his shoulder. "Seriously, Maddux, who did this?"

"Work."

I took his jacket and let him sit. "You can't tell me?" I knew he had a job that could get rough, but to see him battered and bruised might take a toll on my mental health.

He pulled me into his chest and hugged me. "We had a lead and got into an accident."

"Are you hungry?"

He shook his head and kissed my shoulder. "How is the baby?"

"Fine, but you're more important right now."

Maddux pulled back and brought me around to the couch and sat me in his lap. "What did you do today?" Our fingers locked together.

"Hung out with Rose and Vanessa."

"Did you cook?"

I went to get off his lap. "No, but I have leftover food from lunch." A part of me was wondering if I would have weird cravings, since I had gained a few extra pounds.

He dragged a hand up my thigh. "Just stay here. I like you this close."

I ran my index finger across his bottom lip. "What are we doing, Maddux?" I muttered as his eyes opened and closed slowly.

Maddux brushed his nose against mine, then inhaled my scent. "You tell me."

"*Warf!*"

Maddux's nose wrinkled in confusion. "What's that?"

I gestured to my bedroom. "Princess. Ignore her and tell me about the accident."

"That's a story for another day. Did you get the money for the baby?"

Maddux wanted to make sure I had everything I needed, so he opened an account that I could use when he wasn't around. I leaned in closer and grazed my lips over his. He opened his mouth a little more, and I sucked on his tongue.

Maddux moved his hand to my belly. "You're starting something."

I teased with a curt smile, rubbing across his chest. "It's the baby."

He tangled his fingers in my hair. "Where's your bedroom?"

"In the back?" I shuddered in his hands from the feel of his mouth.

"*Warf!*" Princess barked.

"We can let her out." I stood and grabbed his hand.

He walked up behind me, wrapped his arms around my waist, and peppered kisses along my neck. I pushed open the door, and Princess ran out of the bedroom. Maddux stepped around me. I watched as he scanned my bedroom, then removed his shirt and jeans and kicked off his shoes. I slid my pants and shirt to meet him halfway. He squeezed my hand, closing the space between us.

"You're even more beautiful with the swell of your hips."

"Thank you."

"I still have the memories of our night on the boat."

He cupped my chin and leaned down, claiming my lips. Then lifted me up by my legs, and I wrapped my arms around his neck as we kissed hungrily.

"Are we crazy for doing this?" I whimpered as he gently lowered us to the bed. I opened my legs as he dropped his boxers.

"It would be crazy to ignore that I want you and feel a connection I can't explain."

Maddux's eyes roamed over my belly. He bent down, his muscles flexing, and layered kisses around my stomach up to my breasts, slowly flicking his tongue around my nipples. That caused me to bolt off the bed. He gently rubbed up and down my thigh. The chemistry between us was electrifying. My pussy spasmed, as he lifted my leg and slid his thick member into me. My breath hitched.

"Maddux," I cooed, brushing my hand down his back.

"Shit!"

He was steady with his strokes, while he lined our mouths together. I enjoyed the warmth of his body, yet he kept his distance to not put pressure on my belly. This was us making love and coming together. We weren't strangers anymore.

"Oh... Ahhh!" I slammed my hand on the bed.

Maddux released my lips and pushed my legs up to my chest. I rubbed a hand up and down his arms. His large hand gripped my legs, commanding ownership.

"Maddux, fuck!" I cried as I felt my juices spurt onto his stomach and down my thighs onto the sheets. He swiftly pulled out and bent down to capture my throbbing lower lips, stare into my eyes. I shuddered as he sucked on my clit and used his hand to caress my breast. I brushed a hand on the back of his head as he lifted up and pushed back inside me, placing light kisses on my neck and nuzzling his face in my neck. He clapped a hand around my waist and sped up his strokes.

"Baby! Yes. I'm coming," I cooed, goosebumps covering my skin.

"Keep me on a high, baby. Right behind you... ugh... fuck," he moaned.

I gasped as I came for the second time, my eyes rolled back, and I wiggled my hips as my breath hitched.

He froze as he released inside me. "Hmmmm..." His mouth slowly moved away, and we both came up for air.

I placed a hand on his chest as we lay together. "Are you staying tonight?" I slung a leg over his thigh.

We faced each other on the bed.

Maddux took a deep breath. "I had no plans of leaving." Warm fingers brushed over my face.

I grinned and started to get up, but he stopped me, kissed me on the forehead, and tapped me on the thigh.

"Where's your bathroom?" His biceps were ripped with tattooed designs.

I pointed around the corner of the hallway.

"Stay here, I'll get a towel to clean you up. Then we can eat."

I grazed a hand over his full length. "I'm not hungry for food."

His eyes rose in surprise. "Then I guess we can wait to clean up."

I leaned up, grabbed his erect dick, pulled it into my mouth, and showed him what I could do.

Chapter 10

Chanel

The next morning
He released his hold around my waist and slid down, trailing kisses up my left thigh. Moving back up to my face, he pecked me on the check. I rubbed a hand over my pregnant belly, snuggled up close to his warm, hard body, tossed my leg over his, and reached to hug him around the waist as we clasped our lips together.

"I have to get going."

I grumbled and removed my arm. "I hate that you have to leave." I blew out a breath, leaned up on my elbows, and watched him climb out of bed.

"When are you coming visting again?"

"In a few weeks, once I get work situated."

"Stop frowning."

"Are you going to tell me about this?" I sat up on my knees on the edge of the bed and touched the wound above his eye.

He pulled the shirt over his head. "I met up with Aydin and the guys. It went from a surveillance to a chase."

I watched Maddux slide his feet in his shoes and button

his pants. "How much longer is it going to take to get this guy?" There was something familiar about this moment, except this time, Maddux stood next to me the next morning after our all-consuming session in bed.

He gripped my elbow, turned to face me, and pecked my lips. He scanned the time on his watch and cursed. "I have to go."

"Be safe." I pointed at my stomach. "For this little one."

He caressed my cheek. "Is that the only person worried about me?"

I threw myself against his chest and wrapped my arms around his neck. "Both of us want you safe."

"There is something I want to talk to you about when you come to Collierville."

"What?"

He released his hold and shifted.

"I saw the nursery, and I understand you want to work, but you should think about Collierville as a place to lay the foundation."

"What do you mean?"

"Your family is in Collierville, so is my family and my work."

I stopped at the door, opening it as he rubbed my shoulder. "My life is here."

"Again, I understand. But with everything happening with Rayo—"

I raised my hand to cut him off. "Are you saying I'm in danger?" Alarm and anger rippled along my spine.

Maddux stood firm, gripping me by the shoulders. "Chanel, I wouldn't let anything happen to you, trust me."

"But..."

"My interest in you living in Collierville is more for me to be closer to you and our baby."

"That's a big step."

He kissed me on the forehead. "Never would I put you in a situation that would hurt you. My feelings are real."

I closed the door and leaned against it with my eyes closed, running a hand over my stomach. "What do you think, baby? About Collierville." I spoke to myself and rose from the door when my phone rang showcasing Erica my coworker.

"Hey Chanel, sorry to bother you."

I headed to feed Princess. "What's going on, Erica?"

"The reports for Rogers and Field need to be sent off, and I don't have the final numbers."

I turned on the faucet and filled her bowl. "Why do you need the final numbers? The account isn't finalized."

"Well, I just got a call that he's moving to another company."

I leaned on the counter. "Wait! What did Rogers do?"

"Yeah. They want the final numbers so they can get a new company."

I ran a hand down my face. "Why am I just hearing about this?" I grabbed my laptop off my desk and logged into my account.

"You know the boss didn't want to throw more work at you," Erica explained.

"That's not a decision he should make without speaking to me first," I fussed, clicking into my account.

"Do you want to send me everything, and I'll have him call you?"

"I'll be in the office. Give me twenty minutes."

"Sounds good."

I hung up and dropped my phone on the couch, looking over the accounts. Most of them were updated with new account holders.

"Bastard."

The audacity to try to push me out and use me being pregnant as an excuse. I hopped up and rushed to shower so I could get over there before anything was finalized.

* * *

The elevator was crowded as I stepped off. I stomped down the hallway to my boss' office and pushed the door open without waiting for an answer. He was in a meeting with a young woman.

My boss Joey jolted up. "Chanel!"

"I need to talk to you," I demanded, not letting him get away with a brush-off.

Joey's eyes moved toward her and back to me. "Can this wait?" He fluffed some paperwork.

I glanced at her and back to my boss. "No." I took my work seriously and the audacity to pull a stunt aggravated me.

He sighed and gestured to his guest. "Lourdes, do you mind excusing me for a minute?"

"No problem," she replied, and my boss stepped around his desk.

"Why am I getting a call that my accounts are being pushed to other people?" I spat, crossing my arms over my chest.

He motioned to step out of his office. "Chanel, you're a great accountant, but the amount of things surrounding you are hindering your productivity."

"That's bullshit!" I barked, seeing him as the true asshole he had become.

"Have you met with your top clients these past few weeks? What about signing onto the global conference?"

I didn't have an answer for him, and I hated to admit that my mind had been on other things lately. "Look, my job is what I love, and you're taking it away from me."

He folded his hands together in front of him. "I don't doubt you love the work, but I need someone to commit one hundred percent."

"So, almost dying doesn't mean anything?" I spat out the words contemptuously.

"That's not what I said. Lower your voice." He looked around the office as people focused on us. "Erica is going to take your accounts. Take a vacation and focus on yourself. When you're ready, come back."

I started to storm out and chucked my head back in frustration. "No, thank you."

Joey ran after me, grasping my hand. "So, you're not willing to compromise?"

I pointed a finger in his face. "Why should I when I brought over a hundred million in clients?"

Joey turned, heading back to his office. "Chanel, I have a client waiting. We will discuss this another time."

The woman named Lourdes came out holding a phone up to ear. They said their goodbyes, and she walked to the elevator.

"Chanel, what are you doing here?" Moria wondered.

I pointed at Joey's office, then sauntered to the elevator.

Moria followed me to the elevator. "What did he say?"

Moria followed me to the elevator.

I waited for the door to open. "What I've been thinking all this time. He's trying to get me out."

Moria crossed her arms, facing Joey's office. "Did he say that?"

"Basically, but whatever. I'm going on vacation."

"Where are you going?"

She stopped the doors from closing.

"Collierville."

* * *

A month later in Collierville

My father threw a little party for my visit today. I told him I didn't want anything extra, but Dad couldn't stop when it came to spoiling me. Now that his first grandchild was coming, there would be even more spoiling. His words, not mine.

When word got out that I was here, we almost had an entire family reunion. I needed peace and quiet, so he made sure to keep visitors to a minimum. Like right now, there were about twenty guests. Maddux was invited not only because I wanted them to finally meet him, but as our relationship grew stronger and I was further in my pregnancy, I wanted him close.

Dad brought me a plate of food. "He's a good pick."

Maddux taught the kids how to play basketball on a plastic toy my dad set up for the kids.

"I'm happy you approve."

Dad bent down and kissed me on the forehead. "Your mom would approve."

I cocked my head to look in his eyes. "You think she would?"

Dad chuckled, holding up his hands. "Well, the way it happened, I doubt that would have been our first choice, but you're a grown woman."

I chuckled at the awkwardness of him hearing I got knocked up from a one-night stand. "Believe me, this wasn't something I planned."

His eyes roamed back over to Maddux. "Have they caught the guys who tried to rob you?"

"Maddux told me they're still on the loose, but they have leads." I shoved more food in my mouth.

"He protects you. That's what I've always wanted for you."

I picked through the potato salad. "I know, Daddy."

"Now what's happening with your job?"

I dropped the fork on my plate and put it on the table next to me. "Lost my appetite."

He sipped on his beer. "You're eating for two now."

I picked up the bottle of water and drank it. "Joey is being an ass and basically, I put in my notice." My dad would be ready to go and kill Joey with just a word for hurting his baby.

"Did he say you should quit or take some time while you're pregnant?"

"He didn't get into details, but I always knew he was pushing me out."

He gestured at me. "If he hurt you, know that's his ass."

Maddux walked up and kissed me on the shoulder. "Who hurt you?" He sat next to me on the bench.

"Her boss," Dad hissed.

"Nobody," I groaned. The last thing I needed was both of the men in my life killing Joey.

Maddux lifted my chin. "Don't lie to me, Chanel."

"I'm not, Maddux."

"Did she tell you her boss gave her accounts to someone else?" Dad asked, removing his phone to check messages.

Maddux looked at me, annoyed. "No, she hasn't told me." He kissed my palm.

"There's nothing to tell."

"Says who?"

"Have you eaten?" I tried to change the subject.

Dad laughed and rose from the bench. "Just like your mother. Don't let her confuse you, man," Dad told Maddux and pat him on the back.

"Old man is nosey."

Maddux pressed a kiss on my lips and turned my head around to stare into his eyes. "Explain."

I dropped the napkin on the table and recalled everything Joey and I talked about. "Joey's being an ass. I busted in on him having a meeting after getting a call from a coworker."

"What was the call about?"

I shrugged. "He took my accounts away, that's all I know."

"Can he do that?"

I nodded, released a sigh. "Yeah, and I just relayed my frustration with him."

"Give it some time. After the baby is born, maybe call him."

"I will. I refuse to give up what I've built."

Maddux hugged me around the neck. "I like your family."

"They love you more than me." I had rolled my eyes when my aunts and cousins tried to flirt with him earlier.

Maddux tapped me on the nose playfully. "I only have eyes for you."

I poked my tongue out. "I know."

Maddux rubbed my leg. "Forget about everything else and let me take care of you tonight."

"Ooh, and how are you going to take care of me?" I perked up, crossing my legs.

Maddux bent down and sucked on my neck and

pressed a kiss to my earlobe. "A long bath, massage, and my hands all over your body."

"I think I like that idea, Mr. Hayes."

He smashed his lips on top of mine, then slipped his tongue through with a sexy groan. "I knew you would."

We both burst into laughter, and I continued to listen as he talked about his family and the plans for the doctor's visit.

Chapter 11

Maddux

"I am about to be a father," I mumbled to myself and fell on the couch, running my left palm across my head. I'd never even thought about the possibility of having kids, and now I was about to be a father. The last few days, Chanel had stayed between my place and her father's after I got to know everyone.

Ring!

"Fuck!" I grabbed my phone from my pocket and noticed my mom was calling. I had briefly talked with them, but not much because of tracking down Rayo and his crew.

"Hello," Mom said.

I pressed my lips together and cleared my throat. "Hey, Ma." The TV replayed the robbery with Rayo from the last few weeks. For the last few nights I watched footage and read up on his team to get a better handle on how to approach things.

"I dreamed about fish last night." My mom liked to think she was one of those parents who was a friend, but she's a little old school when she tried to be in our business on dating.

I groaned and scrubbed a hand down my face, leaned my head back to rest. "Ma."

"Tell me now if I'm going to be a grandmother."

"I-I—" I stuttered.

"Micah!" she yelled for Dad.

I sat up. "Ma, calm down."

"We're going to be grandparents!" she shouted, and I heard clapping in the background.

"Who's pregnant?" Dad asked.

"Maddux. Who is she and don't lie?" Mom pressed.

I stood, trekked into the kitchen, popped the fridge open, and grabbed a beer. "What makes you think someone is pregnant?"

"A woman knows," Mom answered.

I gulped it down, tossed the cap in the trash, and lingered at the counter. "Well, I was waiting to talk to you in person." I could see it now. Our child would be with them and never come home if we let them. He or she would be spoiled rotten.

"Who is the girl?" Mom checked.

"Her name is Chanel, and we met through friends." I could no longer hold out on any information, I just hoped they understood this was my life and Chanel was a part of it no matter if they liked or not.

"Why does it sound like you two aren't a couple?"

I grabbed another beer and watched Princess come into the kitchen like she worked a long day at the job and was ready for dinner. "We weren't at the time."

"So, are you a couple now?"

I turned the faucet off after filling the bowl, then placed it on the mat. "Uhmm... it's something like that."

"Tell me something, Maddux, because I know this wasn't one of your little floozies you've gotten knocked up," Mom sassed. She'd hated the women I'd dated in my past.

"Ma!"

"Give me the phone, Maise." She argued with my dad then there was rustling on the other end.

As my stomach rumbled, I decided to make something to eat while they went back and forth. I laid my phone down and clicked over to speakerphone. I removed sub bread and condiments, then a bag of chips and plates.

"Son," Dad said.

"Yeah, Dad."

"What is your mother talking about? Some girl is pregnant?"

I dipped the knife in mustard and filled both sides of the bread. "Man, Pops, I slipped up."

"So, it's true. You're going to be a father?"

Finally, I sliced the sub in half and poured some chips on the side of the plate. "We have to go to the doctor tomorrow to find out if it's a girl or boy."

"After the doctor's office, I want you to bring her over for dinner," he insisted.

I bit into the sandwich, then washed it down with my beer. "I'm not sure about that." Chanel might want to spend time with her dad. As an only child I knew how much she meant to him. I never wanted to cut into their bond and this was a special time for her.

"Why?"

I sat down on the stool at the island. "It's too early. I mean we still don't know anything about each other."

"You knew enough to sleep with her."

"I see where this is going," I grunted, wiping off my mouth.

"Like I said, bring her over," he demanded.

I sighed and sipped on the rest of the beer. "Fine. Tell Ma to not be all crazy." I scanned the TV as a movie popped up.

"You tell her yourself." He usually had my back.

I tossed up my arms in aggravation. "Pops!"

"What did you want to say to me?"

I chuckled and pushed my plate away. "Nothing, Ma."

"Good, I can't wait to see my soon-to-be daughter-in-law."

"All right, you're doing a little too much right now, crazy lady." At the end of the day my parents wanted the best for me and I knew they had my back, so I let her do what she did best and try to make sure her kids were safe.

"Don't forget dinner's at seven," she said.

"Yes, ma'am." Princess laid at my feet and I bent down to rub her back. Princess was just as territorial over Chanel as my mom was over me.

"Your brother is coming."

"Of course, make it a family reunion." I ended the call then went to change and head to the gym to work off some steam before I stressed myself.

* * *

The next day, I called Chanel to check in on her before I had to pick her up to go to the doctor's office. I told her about dinner at my parents'. At first, she was hesitant. I couldn't blame her, these were strangers. But my parents insisted on meeting her, and I wondered if her father felt the same way about them.

Chanel sat in the chair after checking in with the receptionist. "I'm nervous." Chanel wore a simple blue dress that hugged her curves.

"Me too."

Chanel scrolled on her phone. "Not about the baby. Your parents."

I turned to look at her, rubbed my beard, and nodded in agreement. "Same."

"Do you think they'll accept my baby?" She flipped through a magazine.

"Our."

Her brows creased together in confusion. "What?"

"It's our baby."

After she dropped the magazine in the seat next to her, she clasped her hand on top of mine. "Sorry, our baby."

I sat back in the chair, moved my arm to the back of her chair, pulled her in close, and kissed the top of her head. "If they accept you or not, it doesn't matter."

"How come?"

I smirked and gestured between us. "We're the two people who had sex, so it's our responsibility."

She reared back, biting her bottom lip. "I don't want to come between you and your family."

I placed my hand on her thigh. "You're not. Stop stressing." I lifted her chin and pecked her on the mouth.

"Chanel Forrest," the nurse called her name, and we stood, following her to the back.

She pushed the door open, and Chanel went inside. The nurse told her to change and sit up on the chair for the doctor to examine her. "The doctor will be right in to see you."

"Thanks."

"What are you hoping for?" she questioned.

"Honestly, I just want you and the baby to be healthy."

Chanel nodded.

The door opened, and her doctor walked in and smiled. "Chanel, it's good to see you. How are we doing today?"

"Hi, Doctor Shaw," Chanel replied.

"So, I hear you two want to find out the sex?" Dr. Shaw asked.

"Yes."

Dr. Shaw held her clipboard. "This must be the father?"

I stood near Chanel. "I am." I held my hand out for a shake, then rested in the chair.

Dr. Shaw had to be in her late forties or fifties. She reminded me of an older Vanessa Williams with locks in her hair.

"We'll do a few tests to check in on you first and then confirm the sex," Dr. Shaw explained, typing on her screen.

"Okay," Chanel answered, kicking her feet back and forth.

Dr. Shaw sat in her chair. "Let me have you sit back, and I'll grab my monitor."

I watched as she gathered all her items, and I reached over to grip Chanel's hand. A few minutes went by, and I heard a noise coming from the monitor.

"What's that?" I probed, pointing at the screen.

"That's the baby's heartbeat. Let me check a few measurements," Dr. Shaw spoke, focusing on adjusting her movements.

I tightened my hold on Chanel's hand.

"You're a little around five months," Dr. Shaw expressed, smiling as she moved her hand around.

"Wow! It's coming together for real," Chanel said.

Dr. Shaw asked, "Ready to see what you're having?"

Chanel and I looked at each other.

"Yes," we answered at the same time.

"Well, Mommy and Daddy, you're having a little handsome boy."

She smiled and turned toward us, then pointed at the screen show the outline of our baby.

"A boy," I whispered in disbelief.

Dr. Shaw removed the wand from Chanel's stomach. "Make sure you stay on top of your vitamins." She moved over to her clipboard.

Chanel wiped the tears that trickled down her cheek. "I didn't even know I was pregnant for the first two months."

I pecked her on the cheek.

"That happens sometimes with women, but the baby is healthy," Dr. Shaw said.

"Thank you, Dr. Shaw."

"Have you had any problems, Chanel?" Dr. Shaw asked.

Chanel gripped my hand. "No, besides a few weird cravings." Chanel's priority had been no stress, and I wanted to support her in any way possible.

Dr. Shaw tossed her gloves away. "Okay that's normal. Stay on top of your rest and keep your stress down." Dr. Shaw pushed away from the computer.

"So, the baby is fine even though she didn't know for a few weeks before her visit with you?" I challenged, wanting to know if we needed to do anything extra. I wasn't around when she discovered it, and I didn't plan on missing out on anything else.

Dr. Shaw pat her hand. "Perfectly healthy, continue doing what you normally do and take vitamins."

Chanel sat up and wiped off her stomach. "Thank you, Doctor." She reached for her clothes and I helped her to stand.

"Anytime, Chanel. Make an appointment with the front

desk." Dr. Shaw printed out the pictures and passed them to us.

Not long after we headed out to make a follow-up appointment.

I held the car door open for Chanel. "What are you thinking about?"

Chanel looked at the pictures in amazement. "I'm still in shock but happy, if that makes sense."

I went around the driver's side and hopped in locking my seatbelt.

Ring!

I slipped the key in, revved the engine, and backed up. "This is the guys. Let me take this," I said, putting the phone on speaker.

"Maddux, we just got word that Rayo is here," Aydin explained.

I put on my turn signal and left the parking space. "Where is the location?"

"Word got back that he's looking for revenge on you," Aydin informed me.

A loud gasp left Chanel's mouth.

"You're not alone?" Aydin asked.

"I have dinner plans with my parents. Let me call you back once we finish. My family's safety is priority." I hung up and ran a hand down my face and sighed.

Chanel adjusted in her seat to face me. "Is that about the robbery on the boat?"

I reached over the seat to grasp her hand. "Nothing to worry about."

"How can you say that, Maddux? Someone wants to kill you."

Hoping to ease her mind, I pressed a kiss on her palm.

"That'll never happen." A car honked behind us and I stared in the rearview mirror and checked my surroundings.

Chanel bit her nail and gripped the sonogram. "I guess this is what Bria was talking about." Chanel's nervousness creeped in and I hated that she had any doubts of me protecting her.

"What do you mean?"

"Having someone who works a dangerous job."

"You never have to worry about me."

Chanel twisted the knob on the radio and set it on a jazz station. "We have a child coming, Maddux. I know we're not together, but our child shouldn't suffer."

"For right now, we need to just worry about what color our son's room is going to be." Today was special and I wanted to keep any mention of my job or Rayo away from this moment.

"I already picked the colors of his room." Her excitement perked up and made me feel good about how excited she was over our baby.

"Without talking to me?" We finally pulled up to my parents' house.

"I mean, to be fair, I didn't know you would be interested in stuff like that."

I parked and turned off the car. "How about we get through this dinner, and everything else can wait."

"Sure." As she went to open the door, I placed a hand on her shoulder.

I pecked her cheek. "Never open a door around me." After I climbed from car, I walked around, pulled the handle on her door, then eased my hands down to her ass, and smirked.

The front door of my parents' house opened. I stepped

back and turned. We both waved at Mom then I palmed her stomach, amazed at the shape.

"Maddux, let that girl loose. You've done enough." My mom was already taking Chanel's side.

Chanel giggled, dipping her head onto my shoulder.

I gripped her wrist and walked up to my mom, kissing her on the forehead. "Funny, crazy lady."

Mom grinned and reached out to hug Chanel. "So nice to meet you."

Chanel stepped forward to give Mom a hug. "Nice to meet you as well, Mrs. Hayes."

Mom captured Chanel's arm, interlocked them, and sauntered inside. "Come inside. How was the doctor's visit?"

Chanel passed the photos to my mom, and she smiled. "Another boy?"

We both nodded at the same time.

"Yeah, so you're still outnumbered," I joked.

Mom wiggled her shoulders and cupped my chin. "That's okay. My baby is worth it."

Chanel gazed at the pictures and artwork. "You have a lovely home, Mrs. Hayes." Chanel smiled.

"Honey, stop calling me that and come sit down. Just call me Mom."

My head turned swiftly at her comment. "Ma."

"Hush, Maddux," Mom chastised.

"I know this may be confusing for you. Maddux and I just met a few months ago," Chanel explained.

Dad came in from the back with a beer in his hand.

Mom took a seat on the edge of the couch next to Dad. "Chanel, this is my husband Micah. I can't lie, we were shocked when Maddux told us but honestly, I had a dream about fish."

"Fish?" Chanel repeated, with widened eyes.

Mom showed Dad the photos. "It's an old tale that when someone dreams of fish, someone is pregnant. And I know his brother doesn't have kids coming."

"Like I told Maddux, at first I had no clue I was pregnant, it was a surprise for sure."

"Well, honey, you have to learn early on in the Hayes family, we come as a package deal now that we know," Mom emphasized.

"That means she's going to be annoying you every minute," I blurted out.

Mom glared at me. "Ignore my son. I cooked dinner, hopefully you like beef stroganoff." Dad chuckled, and Mom smacked him on the arm.

Chanel sauntered next to my mom. "I do." They continued to chat like old friends.

I stayed behind with Dad.

"She's beautiful."

"I got a call from Aydin."

Dad held the photos toward me and I waved him off. "A case?"

"Yeah, a big time gun smuggler is looking for me. You keep one of the photos."

Dad sat forward, placing his beer on the coaster. "Do we need to have protection?"

"I don't think he's stupid enough to do anything."

He crossed his arms and stared at me. "Be honest with her." Like father like son. We're protectors of the women in our lives and now that a child was coming I knew he'd keep his eyes open for Mom and my girl.

"Chanel was just a one-night stand, and now we're about to be parents. I never want to put her in harm's way, especially our child."

Dad rose from the chair and clapped me on the shoulder. "That's life, son." Dad held the back of my neck.

"Thanks for the advice."

He pat me on the chest. "I'm proud of you. Some men would ignore her and skip out on their responsibilities."

"You raised us to be men, Dad."

"I did, and you've followed my advice. Sometimes your kids have to make their own decisions and as parents, we pray you stay on track."

"Micah!" Mom yelled out for him.

He chuckled after our hug. "Let's go in here and deal with your momma."

"She's going to be worse as Chanel gets further in the pregnancy."

Dad smacked me on the back of the head and laughed. "Stop talking about my wife." Dad loved to spoil Mom and would do the same for my child, so he couldn't really talk.

"Ouch."

Chapter 12

Chanel

Two weeks later

Dinner at his parents' house went great, and we'd been in constant communication since. His mom was sweet and funny, and called or texted with different ideas for a baby shower. I told her I didn't need one, but she insisted on throwing one for me. Since I hadn't been back to Pleasantville, I decided to continue my vacation and ignored calls from Joey. I found out from Moria and Erica she was taking on a lot because Darlene messed up a few clients' accounts and some were leaving the agency.

Maddux stood at the door of his bathroom. "What time is Rose coming to pick you up?" He licked his lips and stared at me as I ran the towel across my breasts.

I stepped back and gestured to stay away. "Get that look off your face."

"What look?" A cocky smile appeared to let me know he was ready for more.

I burst into laughter and shook my head. "That look."

Sex with Maddux was incredible, and being pregnant made it even better, but it left me exhausted afterwards.

Maddux closed the space between us and flicked my nipple. "We won't be late."

"Yes, we will, and your mother will kill me," I moaned and tossed my head back as he peppered kisses along my neck and shoulder.

Ring!

"That must be Rose."

I dropped the blow dryer and ran out of his bathroom to my phone and saw her name scroll across the screen. "Hey, I'm almost ready."

"Great, I should be there in five minutes," Rose responded.

I looked up at Maddux and blew a kiss. "Have you seen the decorations?"

"Yes, and you'll love everything," Rose answered.

"Okay, let me finish getting ready."

"Turning on the street now," Rose explained and ended the call.

I dropped the phone on the nightstand and picked up my dress from the bed, along with my underwear, and slipped them on.

Maddux stepped from the bathroom with the vanilla body oil I used. "Is that Rose?"

"She's parking now." He poured some in his hand and rubbed my arms.

Maddux dropped to the floor and picked up my leg to rub each foot and thigh. "I'll be right behind you."

"Did you invite the boys?"

He kissed my knee and winked at me. "I did, and they promised to be on their best behavior."

I slapped him on the chest and tittered, "That goes for you too, Mister."

"It turns me on when you take charge."

"No role-playing for you."

Maddux covered my mouth with his lips and gripped my thigh before pulling back. "You caught that."

I burst into laughter and kissed him on the lips. "I see everything." I motioned to my shoes. These days I could barely see my feet with my growing belly.

He tapped me on the ass and helped me slide into my sandals. I put on a little foundation and lipstick and finished my hair in a tight bun after drying.

Knock!

"I got the door." Maddux rose up and trekked out of the bedroom.

"Thanks, babe."

I heard them talk as the steps of Rose's heels hit against the floor. She came into the bedroom all dressed up. "Sexy momma," Rose said.

"You look pretty."

"I clean up nice, right?" Rose danced in a circle.

Maddux came in and hugged me. "My brother's outside, babe. I'll see you there."

"Okay. Be safe please."

He blew a kiss, lifted his wallet, slipped it in pocket, and headed out. "Always."

"Did you meet his brother?" Rose asked.

I snapped my lipstick closed, then sprayed on a little perfume. "Yeah, he's nice, and his fiancée is cool." The Hayes family had really embraced me and I appreciated the welcome.

"Damn, all the fine men are taken." Rose snapped her fingers and sat on the chair in the corner.

I put the second diamond earring in my ear and spun around in the mirror. "Your time is coming."

"Where's your purse?"

"On the dresser."

"Perfect! Let's chop-chop before we are late." Rose got out of the chair and walked out of the room.

I followed, turned the light off, and looked around to see if I missed anything. We stepped out of his house and I locked up. I felt like a million bucks even with swollen ankles. The sun shone, there was a light breeze, the birds chirped, and I had a shawl if I needed. We climbed in Rose's car and she sped to the dining hall his mother rented. My stomach fluttered as time went on, and I felt my baby kicking more and more.

"Here we are," Rose called out and turned into the parking lot of Spector Dining Halls.

I removed my seatbelt and saw all the cars parked out front. "This is nice."

The place had a row of buildings like a shopping mall with different surrounding businesses. I helped Rose grab the bags and she locked the doors behind us.

Rose swung her hips left to right. "I'm so ready to eat and drink."

"This looks expensive."

"Maddux said not to spare a penny."

"Really?" I picked up my pace as best as I could, scanning the crowded parking lot.

Rose held the door open for me. "That man loves you."

"Here she is!" Maise smiled and sauntered toward me with her arms open.

I let her go and held up the bags. "Hi, Maise."

The large sign in the front had our name etched in gold and pictures of us as kids. Music played. The hall was lined up with tables and name badges and a sign in booklet.

Maise gripped my hand. "Let me grab the boys to take these. Come and look at everything." She waved over Maddux and his brother.

"What do you think?" Maddux asked, placing his hands around my waist.

"Everything looks beautiful, baby." I saw some of the guys across the room, they walked up to us. I had met Amelia, his wife a few days ago, and Bria brought her baby along.

"I told Maddux we'd pull this off. We have games and food." Maise's excitement shone in her talkative state. His father tried to get her to relax, but she wouldn't sit for a moment.

"How many single women are here tonight?" Soaquan asked, and we burst into laughter. Maise placed the bags in his hands to put them away.

"Between him and Bishop, I can't keep up," Maise said.

"Where's our table?"

"Right over there," Maddux answered and escorted me to the table.

I placed my purse down and smiled at everyone. "Let me run to the restroom really quick."

Ring!

Hearing my phone start up annoyed me. Today was not to be stressful.

"You need me to come with you?" Maddux checked.

I ignored my phone and waved him off. "No, just point me in the right direction."

"Around the corner and down the hall." Rose went over to Bria and Cairo and picked up the baby.

"I'll be right back."

The entire place was in a colorful bears theme. The gift table overflowed with more than we needed. We probably wouldn't need to purchase diapers for six to nine months. They had a DJ, games, and a buffet set up, and I headed down the hall and went into the bathroom, thankful it wasn't crowded. After I flushed, I stepped out and saw a woman at the counter washing her hands, and I smiled.

"Do I know you?" Something about her was familiar.

She extended her hand. "We've met before. I'm Lourdes." Her long hair almost hit her butt.

"Lourdes," I repeated, confused as to where I saw her before.

She hung her head. "Joey."

"Oh, that's where I know you from. How did you hear about this? Did Rose invite you?"

She smiled and reached in her pocket. "Actually, I'm here on behalf of Rayo." She removed her hand and pointed a knife at me.

I stumbled back, covering my stomach as best as I could. "Please don't!"

* * *

The car moved at a high speed, and I wondered where they were taking me. My hands were tied together, and a black cloth was over my head. I felt stupid for not taking extra precaution when Maddux asked to show me to the bathroom. I prayed they knew something was wrong and would come to find me. Trying to fight was out of the question with me being pregnant. These people didn't seem to care if they hurt my child.

"Please, I'll give you anything. Just let me go."

"Shut up!" Lourdes shouted.

"Rayo, I sent the message," another man said.

"He will know soon," a deep voice, who I assumed was the leader, said.

"Maddux will give you whatever you want, just don't hurt me," I pleaded, then I felt a sharp blade poke me in the side.

"Either you shut up, or I'll make you shut up," she snapped.

"Lourdes, calm down. I have plans for her," Rayo growled.

I froze at his words. We continued to drive, and I hoped to God I made it home safe.

"We'll set her up as bait and kill him," Rayo informed them.

My mouth dropped open, and a chill ran up my spine.

"Are we almost there? I'm tired of being around her. If it's not you, then it's every other guy wanting to sleep with this broad," Lourdes complained.

Slap!

"Shut the fuck up, Lourdes! I run the show!" Rayo yelled.

Lourdes nudged the knife in my side a little harder. "Fuck you, Rayo!"

Pop!

I gasped and felt a trickle of pee run down my leg.

"Stupid bitch," Rayo growled.

The car finally stopped, and the door opened. I felt the sun shining on my skin when someone gripped me by the elbow and pulled me out of the car.

"Keep your mouth shut," he demanded, slamming the door.

Suddenly a hand wrapped around my throat. They

pushed me to keep walking. I didn't hear much around me. No cars, yelling, or people talking.

"Move. Go inside." He nudged me forward.

I froze. "I- I- don't want to die."

"Too late." He grabbed me by the arm and forced me to go.

I almost tripped, but he caught me by the arm and waist, and we walked for a few seconds before coming across some steps. He removed the black cloth, and I looked around to an abandoned underground railway station.

I swiped the tears that fell. "Where are we?"

"Nowhere you should worry about. Keep going."

"I can pay you whatever you want." I knew I wasn't rich and Maddux came from a modest family, but I wanted to try and buy as much time as possible.

Rayo cocked his gun and pointed it at me. "Keep walking."

"The other men are pulling in now." His men held a gun and a phone.

"He won't make it inside alive," Rayo taunted, pressing the gun to my back.

Rayo approached an unlocked door, and I stepped into a room with an old chair, desk, and broken light.

"Sit." Rayo shoved me down.

I scanned my surroundings. "Are you going to let me go?"

Rayo dragged the gun down my cheek to my breasts. "I see why Maddux knocked you up. You're a beautiful woman."

"Maybe we should take turns and test her out," Miquel spat.

Miquel and Rayo laughed at his comment.

"I'd prefer to do it in his face. Let him see how much

you wanted Chanel." Rayo gripped my chin and wiggled his tongue at me.

I tried to turn my head, but he forced me to face him. A rat ran by and more piss ran down my leg.

"Ooh, she's a pissy little bitch." Miquel cackled.

"Maddux is going to kill you," I hissed.

Rayo frowned and slapped me across the face.

I had to be brave for my baby and pray Maddux found us soon. Violence never happened in my world, but I wanted Maddux to skin them alive.

Chapter 13

Maddux

I threw the cell phone across the room when I saw a picture of Chanel with a black cloth over her head. "Goddammit!"

"We're going to get her back," Bishop said.

Rayo thought he would get away with this, and I promised to make his life a living hell if he touched a hair on her head.

"What do you got, Columbo?" I called over the speakerphone. I should have known Rayo would try something at the baby shower. I had let my guard down.

"I got an address heading to your phone now," Columbo replied.

"Let's go."

"Maybe you should sit this one out." Cairo stopped me before we rallied the guys out to the cars.

"Did you sit out when Bria was in trouble?"

Cairo smacked me on the chest. "You're right."

He passed me a gun, and I slapped hands with him. Yeah, it was crazy to have these feelings for someone I'd only known for a short time, but I could honestly say I'd grown to love her and my son. When I asked her about moving in with me, it caused our first big fight, but we'd grown closer throughout the process of getting things together for our son.

I hopped in the back of the car.

"You're running things, Maddux. It's your show and your woman," Aydin called from the front seat.

"I want to be the first person she sees."

"We will take them back then," Cairo responded.

The address was to an old, abandoned port authority tunnel that the city closed years ago. I checked the time, and it was still early. Rayo expected us to come alone, and I didn't need the police to help me, but I wanted an ambulance in case something happened with the baby. Cairo was on the phone, arranging for his contacts at the nearest hospital to be ready. My dad understood I needed to leave, but Mom was upset and crying nonstop along with Rose.

We arrived at the destination and parked a few blocks away. Aydin held up the binoculars and watched the area.

I sat forward, stared out of the window, and removed my gun. "What do you see?"

"Two men out front."

I saw one truck parked out front, then pushed my earpiece in to be ready.

"Rayo is probably ready to escape," Cairo remarked.

I went to step out of the car.

"Maddux," Aydin called my name.

"I'm going, Aydin."

Aydin dropped the binoculars and slipped in his earpiece. "I'm not going to stop you but be smart."

Aydin was right. Going in guns blazing would cause harm to Chanel, and I didn't want to stress her out more.

"You take out the shorter one, and I got the one on the

right," I explained to Bishop, and we shut the door, walked up to both men, and raised our hands. The anxiety of what I might find felt like the time stopped on our dreams.

"We're here to see Rayo."

"Guns, drop them," the taller bodyguard with a black eyepatch on his right eye and sleeveless leather jacket demanded, pointing his gun at us.

I dropped my hands to my sides. "Are you going to make this easy on yourself or not?"

He smirked and raised the gun to my face. "You must be after that pretty little pregnant bitch."

The mention of Chanel flipped a switch in my brain, and all I could think about was if they had touched her. I turned my head toward Bishop, Aydin, then Cairo.

"Now!" The motherfucker did the one thing he shouldn't have. I slowly reached behind my back for the gun and went to pass it to him. He released the hold on the trigger, and that was my moment to punch him in the face, grip his wrist, and remove the gun. I didn't have time to see what Bishop or Cairo were doing, but I knew they were safe based on the screams of the other bodyguard.

Pop!

"Arghhh!" He was knocked down and shot in the leg. Aydin took his gun and put it behind his back.

Cairo opened the door and saw it was clear. "You take this way, and we're going to the other side."

I nodded in agreement and let the door close as I heard loud screams.

"Let me *go!*" Chanel yelled.

I wanted to shout at the top of the stairs, but I had to stay calm. "Chanel, I'm coming," I mumbled to myself, darkness surrounded us, it was a cold and damp environment that no pregnant woman should be placed.

"Maddux!" Chanel screamed again.

Ratttttta! Rattttaa!

I ducked to the side of the wall as bullets from an assault weapon came in my direction.

"Let her go, Rayo!" I yelled, then slowly leaned off the wall and aimed my gun in the direction of his men.

"I want my money!" Rayo demanded, and I heard more gunfire.

"Maddux!" Chanel shouted.

Pop! Pop!

I waited a few seconds, and when it went silent, I leaned over to see it was clear. I went toward them and saw Rayo and his team push Chanel to another exit. I sent off a shot, and it struck one of his men in the arm. Rayo turned, looked back at me, and aimed to shoot, but Chanel pushed her elbow in his left side and stepped on his foot. She took off while she held her stomach, and Cairo caught her with Aydin next to him.

I stepped on Rayo's hand before he could pull the trigger. "I wouldn't try that if I were you."

Rayo groaned and released his grip on the gun. "You got this one, but I'll be back."

"Are you sure about that?"

"Fuck you," Rayo hissed.

I put pressure on the wound with my foot. "You fucked with the wrong one."

* * *

Months later

I held my son in my arms and stared at his perfect hands, feet, nose, and lips. Thinking back to the day Rayo kidnapped Chanel, my entire world was in limbo, and I had no clue if I'd have this moment. Chanel talked with Rose, my mom, and her dad as the guys came in one by one to bring in the presents. A one-night stand ultimately brought me the best gift in the world, true love and a beautiful boy.

"Maddux, you have to let someone else hold him," Chanel fussed.

I chuckled, she was just as spoiled as our son would be. "He's fine." I smiled at my baby boy.

"He's going to spoil little MJ," Rose complained and came around the hospital bed, extending her arms to take my son.

I held him close to my chest. "Did you wash your hands?"

Rose reached to grab him. "Yes! Let me hold my godson!"

"What happened to your other friend?"

"Who?" Chanel wondered.

"The one who was on the boat. I think I like her better," I joked, and Rose growled at me.

I handed over my son, and she sat down with him on the chair.

"How long do you have off before your next assignment?" Chanel inquired.

I bent down and kissed her on the forehead, then cheek. "Nothing for you to worry about."

"I don't want you to have to choose." Chanel gripped my shirt and poked out her lips for a kiss.

"Listen, let me worry about that. You focus on yourself and be ready for another one."

I tilted her chin and kissed her on the lips.

"At least let the girl breathe a little," Rose blurted out, and I laughed. We'd grown closer over the past three months, and I knew Chanel loved that her best friend and boyfriend got along. I knew Rose was genuine and in Chanel's corner during good and bad times.

"Who invited her?" I kidded.

Mom popped me on the back of the head. "Maddux!"

Knock! Knock!

The door opened, and Bria walked in with Cairo behind her, carrying a large teddy bear and balloons.

"Hello!" Bria waved at our parents, then went to the side of the hospital bed and hugged Chanel.

"I didn't know you were coming," Chanel said.

Cairo and I hugged. I took the presents out of his hand.

Bria cooed at MJ. "Cairo wanted to wait until you got settled before bringing me up here."

"How is the little one?"

"Amazing, but how are you feeling?" Bria asked.

Chanel held up her cup of water. "Tired, hungry, and ready to take my baby home."

Bria washed her hands and walked over to Rose. "You'll be released tomorrow, so Maddux can spoil you tomorrow."

"I told her we'd have around-the-clock babysitters with our parents."

My mother raised her thumb in acceptance.

"How long was your labor?" Bria asked.

Chanel passed me the cup to refill. "Not long at all. MJ was easy."

Cairo motioned his head to the door, and I sensed something was up.

"I'm going to talk with Cairo, babe. I'll be right back," I told them.

Cairo clapped me on the shoulder as we walked out of the room then looked over his shoulder. "I didn't want to say anything in the room."

I looked back and then faced him. "What's up?" Having a son, I had to know where Rayo was at all times.

"Rayo is going down. All the evidence against him, plus Chanel's kidnapping, is sending him away for life."

I thought back on that day months ago, when I was close to ending Rayo's life. I had to remind myself not to turn into the type of person Rayo expected me to become. I let Aydin take him, and he was arrested when we got out of the tunnel. To my surprise, news reporters surrounded and filmed everything and wanted interviews. My focus was to get Chanel to safety, so I pushed the reporters on Cairo. Rayo was up on charges ranging from kidnapping to murder and robbery, and more. He tried to plead insanity, and they said no.

Cairo cocked his head in Chanel's direction. "How has she been?"

"The first few days she was afraid to sleep, but we've gotten through it. She's a fighter."

Cairo shoved his hands in his pockets. "Glad you've found someone who keeps you balanced."

"I owe her everything, man."

"They make it worth it when you come home."

"Yeah, MJ and Chanel needed me, but I was the one who needed them."

Epilogue:
Chanel

A year later

I held my little bundle of joy in my arms. As she slept, I kissed her tiny little hands. Maddie was the spitting image of me, while Maddux Jr. looked like his father. We decided to have our main home in Hendersonville close to his office, and got a condo in between Downtown Nashville and Collierville for when we visited my dad. At first, I was against moving and leaving my job, friends, and home, but it made sense with his work. His family was supportive of our relationship and my dad surprisingly loved babysitting. He made sure to let Maddux know that he'd kick his ass if he ever hurt me.

"You're so special, Maddie," I cooed and caressed her cheek.

The house was close to Maddux's parents after they moved to be near the kids. I smiled at little Maddux, holding a bag in his hand, mimicking his dad as they brought in more boxes. They dropped them near the front door and he ran off to the living room. Maddux's mom was in the kitchen, cooking lunch for everyone. My dad and Maddux's father were in the living room, watching a game.

I glanced around the kitchen. "Do you need any help?"

Maddux wrapped his arm around my waist and kissed me on the forehead. "You need to relax."

"No, everything is almost done. Listen to your husband," Maise quipped.

MJ held his hands up for his dad to pick him up.

"I feel bad. I didn't help with anything."

Maddux smacked me on the ass. "You just gave birth, Miss Lady."

"Stop that. You know when you say that, it turns me on," I whispered, and he grinned.

"I'd advise you to wait six weeks. You already have two under two." Maise pointed her finger at us.

I passed Maddie off to Maddux. "Tell that to your son, Maise. I tried to tell him." I nuzzled my nose in her neck.

"Has she eaten?" Maddux asked.

"Yeah, I just finished nursing her."

"Oh, Rose called earlier," Maise said.

I walked to the sink to wash my hands and picked up a fork to taste the potato salad. "She did?" I gave a thumbs-up it was good.

Maise nodded, lifted MJ, and put him on the counter to give him a piece of bread.

"I have to call her and check in. It's been a few days since we talked."

Ding!

"Who's that?" I asked.

Maddux shrugged and turned to leave the kitchen. I followed him when he opened the door and got the shock of my life.

"Rose!"

"Chanel Hayes, you go and get married and forget about your friend." Rose dropped her bags on the floor and reached out for a hug.

"When did you get here?"

"About an hour ago. I called to tell you, then figured I would surprise you." Rose released me and went to grab Maddie.

I walked beside her with Maddie. "We have so much to catch up on."

Maddux picked up her bags and took them to the guest room. Rose and I went back to the kitchen.

"Rose, you remember Maise, my mother-in-law."

Rose sat down as Maddie opened her eyes. "Hi, Mrs. Hayes."

"How are you doing, Rose? Are you staying for lunch?"

Rose placed Maddie in her swing. "I took a few days off from work to visit."

"We have plenty of room." I picked up the plate of food and carried it to the dining room.

"She seems so relaxed. Does she sleep through the night?" Rose inquired.

I stepped back in the kitchen. "Maddie's like Maddux Jr. when he was a newborn."

Rose pretended to dance with Maddie's legs and hands. "I'm so happy for you, Chanel."

I leaned my head on her shoulder and grinned. "Thank you for not letting me lose my mind."

"Maddux wouldn't allow that to happen. I still can't believe what you went through."

I fixed Maddie's bib and reached for the chair. "That's in the past. They can't hurt us anymore."

"I'm glad. Maybe I should get a big military man."

I pointed at my hubby. "Talk to Maddux's single friends."

"Who's single?" Maddux quizzed, stretching his arm around my shoulder.

"Rose."

Rose reached for MJ, but he didn't listen and ran away. "I told her I might need to meet a military man so I can have what she has." Rose motioned between the two of us.

MJ ran back in the kitchen and held on to my legs.

I bent down to pick him up. "Baby, you ready to eat?"

"Yes!" He giggled and snuggled his face in my chest.

"Yeah, feed him now and you can feed me later," Maddux whispered in her ear.

Maise clapped her hands together. "Time to eat."

Ding!

"Now who is that?"

Maise saw the door open, and her mouth gaped. "Look who pulled up when we had food on the table." Maise laughed. I looked out of the kitchen and saw Mykelti and his pregnant fiancée Lizzy.

"Looks like a family reunion to me," Maddux said.

I teared up, thinking about my mom as Mykelti laughed and talked with his brother and mom. These moments I'd savor for a lifetime and never regret how I met Maddux. He brought so much more to my life than I could have wished for.

Maddie started to cry, and Rose passed her to me.

"This reminds me of why I don't want kids," Rose said, and everyone burst into laughter.

"You say that now."

"The door is closed to babies," Rose said.

Everyone gathered in the dining room and took a seat. I held Maddie and rocked her to sleep.

About the Author

A TENNESSEE NATIVE and California dreaming Author KeKe Renée is living and striving to continue her passion of writing short story romances in genres ranging from Erotic, Paranormal, and Women's Fiction.

304 Publishing Company

WE SHOWCASE AUTHORS writing African American, Interracial, Women's Fiction, Urban Romance, Erotic, and Contemporary Romance novels. Along with Thriller, Suspense, Poetry, Beauty, and Style Books. Thank you for taking the time out to visit. Join our mailing list to stay updated with new releases and blog posts.

Coming Soon!

Tempt Me: Billionare Boy's Club Book 4
Ravafe Me:: Billionaire Boy's Club Book 5
TN Nashville Division Book 4
TN NAshville Division Book 5

What's Next

Catalogue of Releases By Keke Renée:

•Wet Heat (Wet Heat Series Book 1)

•Every time We Touch Novelette (Wet Heat Book 2 Series)

•His Peace, Her Pleasure

•Baby, It's Cold Outside

•Love Don't Live Here Anymore, Vanessa Andrew Book 1

•Love Don't Live Here Anymore, Isabella Andrew Book 2

•One Night Only-A Novelette (Love By Design Book 1)

•Cassian and Savannah (Love By Design Book 2)

•Deidra's Love (Love By Design Book 3)

•Protecting Bria TN Seal Security Nashville Division Book 1

•Protecting Chanel TN Seal Security Nashville Division Book 2

•Protecting Yanira TN Seal Security Nashville Division Book 3

•Haven

- Taste (A New Adult romance)
- Sensual
- Seek To Please
- Seek To Bare
- Seek To Touch
- Seek To Love
- Seek To Trust
- Seek To Earn

Thank you so much for reading and if you enjoyed the crazy ride and decide to leave a review we'd truly appreciate the support.

Thank you so much for reading and if you enjoyed the crazy ride and decide to leave a review we'd truly appreciate the support.

Catalog of Releases By Chiquita Dennie

Series

<u>Struck in Love</u>

The Early Years-A Prequel Short Story

Ruthless:Antonio and Sabrina Book 1

Savage: Antonio and Sabrina Book 2

Beast: Antonio and Sabrina Book 3

Captivated By His Love:Janice and Carlo

Brutal: Antonio and Sabrina Booke 4

Redemption: Antonio and Sabrina Book 5

<u>Heart of Stone</u>

Broken, Book 1 (Emery & Jackson)

A Valentine's Day Short Book 1.5 Emery & Jackson

Rebirth, Book 2 (Jordan and Damon)

Reveal, Book 3 (Angela and Brent)

Bottoms Up Book 3.5 Jessica and Joseph Short

Renew, Book 4 (Jessica and Joseph)

<u>Cocky Billionaire Boys</u>

Cocky Catcher (Cocky Billionaire Boys Book 1)

Bossy Billionaire (Cocky Billionaire Boys Book 2)

<u>The Fuertes Cartel</u>

Stolen (The Fuertes Cartel Book 1)
Saved (The Fuertes Cartel Book 2)
Betrayed (The Fuertes Cartel Book 3)
<u>Carrington Cartel</u>
Torn: The Carrington Cartel Book 1
Claim: The Carrington Cartel Book 2
<u>Something</u>
Something Gained: A Romantic Comedy Book 1
Something Earned: A Romantic Comedy Book 2
<u>Pierce Motors</u>
Refuel: (Pierce Motors Book l)
Pressure: Pierce Motors Book 2)
<u>Summer Break</u>
Summer Nights: (Summer Break Book 1)
<u>TN Seal Security</u>
Aydin: Book 1
Nasir: Book 2
Nicco: Book 3
<u>Standalones</u>
Until Serena(HEA World Novel)
Temptation
She's All I Need
I Deserve His Love
Mutual Agreement
Scoring with Sadie
Exposed (A Bodyguard Novel)
Love Shorts:A Collection of Short Stories
Red Light District(A Fantasy Romance Short)

Acknowledgments

I can't mention enought the support and dedication of my author buddies for keeping me uplifted. My behind-the-scenes team from beta readers, editors, designers, and more. As a writer I continue to strive for the best, and I appreciate each and every one who reads my work. Without your continual feedback I wouldn't be on this path, letting doubts slip away.

9 781955 233880